EXTRA CREDIT

EXTRA CREDIT

SARINA BOWEN

Tuxbury Publishing LLC

For permissions, contact the author at www.sarinabowen.com/contact

Cover illustration and design by Elle Maxwell.

DEAR READERS

March 2019
Dear Readers,

It's not an exaggeration to say that The Ivy Years changed my life. In March 2014 I was already the author of several books. But The Ivy Years gave me my career, and showed me the path forward.

Readers, thank you so much for supporting me on this journey. It's been a really amazing five years.

All my love,
Sarina

BLONDE DATE

A BLIND DATE. A NERVOUS SORORITY GIRL. A MEAN-SPIRITED FRATERNITY PRANK. WHAT COULD GO WRONG?

As a sorority pledge, there are commandments that Katie Vickery must live by. One: thou shalt not show up for the party without a date. Two: the guy shall be an athlete, preferably an upperclassman.

Unfortunately, Katie just broke up with her jerkface football player boyfriend. Even worse, her last encounter with him resulted in utter humiliation. She'd rather hide under the bed than attend a party where he'll be.

Yet staying home would mean letting him win.

Enjoying herself tonight was out of the question. She could only hope to get through the evening without her blind date noticing that he was spending the evening with a crazy person.

Andrew Baschnagel is living proof that nice guys don't finish first. He's had his eye on Katie since the moment her long legs waltzed into his art history class. So when her roommate sets Andy up to be Katie's date, he'd be crazy to say no. Unfortunately, he doesn't have a lot of practice with either girls or parties. *Yet.*

This story happens during the timeline of The Year We Hid Away.

PART ONE

CHAPTER 1
ANDY

WITH A GROWING SENSE OF PANIC, I pawed through the clothes in my narrow little dorm room closet. For five long minutes I'd stood there inspecting my shirts, tossing them one by one on the bed. That was four more minutes than I'd ever spent before trying to decide what to wear. But I still didn't have a freaking clue.

It was time to call in the big guns.

Luckily, my older sister answered on the first ring. "I need a consult," I said. Delia was in med school, and you got further with her if you spoke in medical terms.

"Where does it hurt?" she asked.

"I have a date, and I don't know what to wear."

Her laughter was so loud that I had to hold the phone away from my ear. "How old are you?"

"Old enough to ask for help when I need it."

"Fair enough. What's the occasion?"

"That's the tricky part. First there's a charity bit, where I'm helping a bunch of sorority girls with their community project. Setting up a Christmas tree, or something."

Delia laughed again. "What do you know from setting up a Christmas tree, Jew boy?"

"How hard could it be? But there's also a tree lighting, and, like, cocktails."

"Hmm," my sister mused. "And where does this event take place?"

"In their preppy white sorority house with the big columns on the front."

"Well… This really could go either way. Casual or dressy."

"That's what I was afraid of. How should I play it?"

"Who's the girl? Anyone special?"

Why yes. But I wasn't going to tell my sister that just hearing this girl's name gave me a thrill. *Katie Vickery.* When she'd called to invite me to this thing, she'd opened with "you don't know me…"

But she'd been wrong. Very wrong. I knew *exactly* who she was.

In the first place, if you were a lonely junior at Harkness, noticing the frosh girls was like your job. And she made my job easy. I'd picked out those long legs the very first time they'd walked into my art history lecture. And — lucky me — summer's warmth had held on an extra week or two this year, treating me to a steady parade of Katie's short skirts every Monday, Wednesday and Friday morning.

The most attractive thing about her, though, was her laugh. It was deeper and huskier than you'd expect from someone so slight and fair. I loved the sound of it. Whenever I heard her laugh, my brain took a short trip around the block.

God, she was hot. But she also had *unattainable* practically stamped on her forehead. Because Katie was the sort of girl that *everyone* noticed. And I wasn't even a little bit surprised when she started sitting with the football crew during lectures.

I didn't dwell on this. Girls like Katie Vickery were out of my league, and I didn't bother to sit around wondering why. Some things just *were.*

As the fall semester wore on, Bridger, my next-door neighbor, started spending a lot of time with Katie's roommate, Scarlet. So I sometimes overheard updates about Katie. Scarlet mentioned that they sometimes went jogging together. After that, Katie's long legs began loping through my dreams in spandex shorts.

But that wasn't a premonition, or anything. It was just the work of a shy guy's subconscious. In a million years, I'd never thought I'd be standing here, dressing for a date with her. And if she hadn't invited me out of sheer desperation, I wouldn't be.

"Um, earth to Andy!" my sister prompted. "I asked you a question. Is the girl anyone special?"

"We don't really know each other," I admitted. "She dumped her football player boyfriend a few weeks ago and needed a date for this thing. Enter me."

"So this is a date of necessity. But how did *you* get the nod? She must not know your track record with women. Not that there's anything wrong with that." My sister snickered.

"Come on, now, D. If I wanted to be mocked, I would have called my *other* sister." Our younger sis was kind of a bitch. "You remember Bridger?"

"Who could forget him?" Delia asked. My neighbor was kind of a stud with the ladies.

"Well, this whole thing was his girlfriend's idea."

"I knew I liked that guy," Delia said. But of course she did. All the women did. "And his girlfriend has good taste, too."

"In me? Or in Bridger?" I teased.

"Both. And this sorority girl is going to love you. You're pretty cute for a skinny guy."

I didn't have time to argue with her. But even if it was true, *pretty cute for a skinny guy* probably wasn't going to be enough to win me Katie's undying affection. I'd been invited on this junket because the newly single Katie was apparently done with football players. "And jerks of all stripes," Scarlet had explained. "I told her, 'Andy is absolutely not a jerk.'"

For a second I'd felt awesome about that. But then I'd realized that being *absolutely not a jerk* also wasn't enough of an endorsement to fill the utter void that was my love life.

Oh, well.

"Are you going to help me or what?" I prodded.

"Of course. So you want to impress her, but you don't want to look like you're trying too hard," my sister said.

"Exactly. So tell me what to wear. While I'm young, if possible."

"Well, when the Jew boy goes to the Christmas tree lighting at the WASPy sorority house, he should always wear nice pants. You have some wool trousers, right?"

I looked at the three pairs I'd draped over my desk chair. "Won't that be too dressy?"

"Not if they're khaki-colored. How about the ones you wore when we saw that show in Boston?"

How did she even remember that shit? If Delia asked me to name three items of clothing that she'd ever owned *in her lifetime,* I couldn't do it.

I lifted the pants off their hanger. "All right. What else?"

"The shirt should be a dark color. Dark blue, maybe? With the collar open. Whatever you do, *don't* button that sucker all the way up. Wear a t-shirt underneath, and it's okay if the t-shirt is visible at the collar. That takes you one notch back toward casual. And no tie."

See? This was why a guy called his sister. I hopped into the pants using one hand. "And the shirt is tucked in, right?"

"Tuck it in! Absolutely. Unless you really don't want to get laid."

I laughed and had to grab the phone to keep it from hitting the floor. "That's not happening."

"Are you saying that because you're talking to your sister? Or because you really believe it?"

"Uh, why? Are you doing a psych rotation at school, or something?" I pulled a clean t-shirt over my head.

"I was only teasing about your record with girls. You know that right? You're a catch, Andy. As long as you tuck your shirt in."

"That must be what I've been doing wrong."

My sister laughed. "Your only real problem is confidence."

I stuffed my feet into a pair of shoes. "Am I wearing a jacket, too? Or just my coat?"

"Your plain black sport jacket. It still fits, right? God, I hope your arms aren't getting any longer. Because you're already kind of like an orangutan."

"And you wonder why I don't have any confidence," I mumbled.

"Kidding! But seriously, if the jacket sleeves are too short, then skip it. And you need to shine your shoes."

"I don't have time."

"What? When is this date?"

"Ten minutes."

"Andrew Isaac Baschnagel! Did you shower and shave?"

"Yes, Mom."

"Hang up and go meet your girl. Crap. I wanted you to send a picture before you left. In case you need tweaking."

"No time for tweaking. Bye, Delia! Thanks."

"Bye, orangutan." Then she clicked off. Delia loved getting the last word.

But never mind. I put on *exactly* what she'd told me to. I hung up the pants that hadn't made the cut. Then, shoving my keys and my wallet into a pocket, I ran out the door and down the entryway stairs. Checking my phone, I saw that I had plenty of time. It was a two-minute walk to Katie's dorm, and I had twice that.

My phone buzzed with a text from Delia. *Good luck with the WASPs, string bean.*

Holding up my phone and grinning like a dork, I took a selfie and sent it to her.

The clothes look great. But UR hopeless, she replied.

That was probably true. And I'd never admit it to my sister, but she wasn't totally off base with her remark about my confidence. Some guys just had a kind of swagger that worked for them. My neighbor Bridger? All he had to do was walk into a room, and the girls hurled themselves at him, like moths at a window screen on a summer night.

But what was swagger, really? It came from the belief that hot girls wanted to take you to bed. So, to acquire it, you'd need at least a little evidence that this was true.

Yeah. I didn't have that. All I had was evidence that a hot girl needed a date for a party. But that was better than nothing, right? And I'd have a couple of hours in the company of the lovely Katie Vickery.

Life could really be worse.

Apparently Delia wasn't done with me, though. When my phone buzzed again, she'd written: *Ask her out on your way home 2nite. Don't chicken out.*

I hadn't thought that far ahead. But my sister was a smart girl. *Okay. If things go well, I'll do it*, I replied.

If U do, I'll buy you a sundae at Lou's. If U chicken out, I win a sundae.

That seemed like a perfectly good incentive to do something that I already wanted to do. *Deal*, I replied.

CHAPTER 2
KATIE

AFTER MUCH DELIBERATION WITH MYSELF, I'd straightened my hair until it hung in golden sheets around my shoulders. It was a kick-ass look on me. Straightened hair said: *I'm here to shine, and I will go that extra mile. So don't you dare mess with me.*

Actually, it probably only said: *I am handy with the straightening iron.* But whatevs. Either way, it gave me confidence, and confidence was in short supply this week.

Unstraightened hair, on the other hand, made a different statement. It said: *I am an effortless beauty, and you'll just have to take me as I am.* But nothing felt effortless lately. And "effortless" was just a little too close to "careless" for my comfort. And tonight I could *not* appear careless. So I'd spent an hour on my hair, and now it was straight enough to be featured on somebody's geometry exam.

I pushed the hair off my bare shoulders and assessed my outfit. "What do you think?" I asked my reflection in the mirror. "Is the neckline too much?"

My reflection didn't answer. But my suitemate Katie did. "There's no such thing as too much. You look hot in that dress."

"Thanks, K2."

"Any time," she said, plopping down on my bed and making herself comfortable.

During the first week of school, a smokin' hot lacrosse player had nicknamed us K1 and K2 because we were both named Katie. "But why does *she* get to be K1?" the other Katie had asked at the time, employing the flirtiest pout *in the world*.

"Sweetheart, K2 is an awesome nickname," the LAX guy said. "Because K2 is a big mountain. And, well…" he broke off on a chuckle, his eyes *right* on her ample cleavage.

The other Katie had grinned, then hitched up her bra. "I guess I can wear that name with pride."

"You wear it well," the guy had said, leaning in to kiss her cheek. About fifteen minutes later, they were lip-locked against a tree in the back yard of the frat house. And I, in my A-cup bra, was totally envious.

And that LAX player wasn't the only one who thought of us as a pair. Our roommate Scarlet called us Blonde Katie (that's me) and Ponytail Katie. Others simply referred to us as The Katies. Together, we'd hit the party scene hard these past three months. I'd begun the year with a kind of I-am-freshwoman-hear-me-roar attitude. I loved college, and it loved me back.

I'd thought so, anyway.

But seven nights ago I'd hit a sour note, and his name was Dash McGibb. Even though I was a generally upbeat person, my bad experience with Dash had left me feeling uncertain about everything — my choices, the company I kept.

This dress.

I fiddled with the silky, draping neckline, wondering if I should change. I probably wouldn't, though. I'd already tried on everything in my closet. Selecting a pink lipstick, I pursed my lips for the mirror.

"I can't believe you're going to this party with a *basketball* player," K2 scoffed from my bed. "The team record so far this season is one for *four*."

The lipstick prevented me from answering her immediately, which was a good thing. It gave me time to reconsider my snarky reply, which would have been to ask Katie how *her* basketball game was looking this year. (She and I ran three miles exactly once per week. Neither of us was athletic. We only jogged on Sundays as penance for our chocolate chip cookie addiction.)

"Is it?" I asked instead. "Then losing is something that Andy and I will have in common. Because my dating record this year is zero for two."

She rolled back onto my bed, her skinny knees pointing the ceiling. "Just because both of your boyfriends turned out to be duds is no reason to sell yourself cheaply."

"*Jeez*, Katie. I'm not a horse up for auction." Her words ricocheted inside my brain. Especially one of them. *Cheaply*. My stomach gave a little lurch at that word. My mother used it a lot. *Cheap* was not how the Vickery women were supposed to behave. But I hadn't heeded this guidance, and now I was paying the price.

K2 gave me a wounded look. "It's just an expression."

"I know. Sorry." I tried to change the subject. "Have you seen my Stila eyeshadow?"

"Um, whoops." She got up and ran off to her own room in our little suite.

The first week of school, I was positive that Katie and I, with our matching names and our matching Prada suitcases, were primed to take over the world. We'd both ruled our high schools. We were also in agreement on exactly which sort of guys we wanted to date — athletes, of course. We were here to party with whoever did it best, and whoever was the best looking.

In contrast, our third roommate, the tight-lipped Scarlet, had seemed a lot less fun. I'm not proud of it, but I'll admit that I'd kind of written her off by the third week of the semester. But recently I'd learned that she'd had damned good reasons to be cautious and quiet. And tonight I found myself wishing that it was Scarlet who was home with me. The attack of insecurity I faced right now was bigger than a fashion crisis. I needed the support of a friend who knew about *life*, and not just what to wear for it.

I hadn't told a soul yet about the crappy little thing that had happened to me last week. And now that I was primping to go to a party where I'd probably end up face-to-face with the jerks who'd embarrassed me, I could have used a pep talk.

K2 came back into my room with my eyeshadow. And when my phone rang, she grabbed it off my dresser to look at the screen. "It's your mom."

"Crap."

"So don't pick up." She did another belly flop onto my bed.

"But I've been ducking her." I took the phone from Katie and answered it. "Hi, Mom."

"Hello, sweetie. Getting ready for your date?"

"I am." *And if you knew that, why would you call me now?*

"I've been making plans for the holidays. We're having the Iversons visit for the weekend before New Year's. And then I thought we could pop into the city to see a play," my mother said.

"Mmm hmm," I said. "Sounds fine." But my attention was still on the full-length mirror I'd installed on the back of our closet door. Specifically, I was trying to decide if the pearl earrings I'd put on made my dress look less slutty. Or had I only managed to convert the look into "slut with pearls"?

"Have fun tonight," my mother said. "Are you wearing something pretty? The girls of Tri Psi knew how to throw a good party in my day."

"Thank you, I will have fun," I said, ignoring the question about my outfit. One had to wonder what my mother's idea of a good college party had been. Surely alcohol didn't enter the picture, at least not for the girls. And my mother would never sanction any activity that might rumple a girl's twin set. Mom was a first-class Good Girl. And in spite of massive evidence to the contrary, she assumed that I was one too.

"Is this boy who's taking you to the party a gentleman?"

"Of course he is," I said. And it might even be true. Though gentlemanliness had never been high on my list of important qualifications for a date.

And last week I'd finally paid the price.

"Good," Mom said.

"Yeah," I said, distracted.

"Say *yes*, darling," my mother corrected. "*Yeah* sounds cheap."

"Yes, Mother," I intoned. "I should go. He'll be here in a minute." At least I hoped he would. It would stink to be stood up tonight of all nights. But after all that had gone wrong this week, I probably wouldn't even be surprised.

I hung up the phone and spun around. "Okay. Last call, here. Are you sure this dress doesn't look slutty?" My fingers worried the fabric between my breasts.

Gently, Katie swatted my hand away. "First of all, we don't use the word 'slutty' when referring to ourselves. And that dress looks *sexy* as all hell. In the best possible way. I hope your basketball player brought a hankie to wipe up his own drool." She got up off the bed and turned me around by the shoulders, so that I was facing the mirror again. "The dress is navy blue, K1. It's an anti-slut color. And the contrast with your hair is just awesome. Use your eyes, babe."

"Thanks," I whispered, trying to see things her way. The dress I'd chosen was cut in a halter style. Until tonight, I hadn't ever stopped to wonder why we were dressing up for this weeknight party, where charity work was supposed to happen, too. But sorority girls, I'd discovered, were always looking for an excuse to get dolled up.

Yet when guys were around (which was always) we were supposed to be grateful if they'd worn khakis instead of sweats, and a button-down instead of a faded Harkness t-shirt. In fact, if they wore their baseball caps frontwards instead of backwards, that was dressy.

Double standard, much?

I dabbed the eyeshadow applicator into the silver shadow and skimmed it across one eyelid and then the other.

Once more I squinted critically at the girl in the mirror. The dress showed a lot of shoulder. But it wasn't too short, which was important. I needed to be able to bend over tonight without giving anyone a show. And the halter top had just enough coverage that I wouldn't expose my cleavage if I leaned forward.

"You look great. Now go," Katie prompted, swatting me on the rear. She gave me a smile in the mirror and slipped out of my room.

I slipped my feet into my most authoritative shoes — black suede Prada pumps with a three-inch heel. Then I took one last look in the mirror. Katie had been right. This dress was perfect. It was sexy without showing off. And my hair looked fabulous, and the jewelry was subtle.

Fine. I looked *fine*. *Not slutty*. I stood there a little longer, willing myself to believe it.

Usually I didn't think so hard about these things. I *liked* to look sexy. And, to be perfectly blunt, I liked sex. A lot. I'd never been afraid to admit that to myself. Not until last week, anyway.

For the most part, coming to Harkness — and getting out from under my conservative parents' roof — had been liberating in all the best ways. In high school, sex had to be sneaky. It's hard to get your freak on when you're listening for footsteps outside your bedroom door. Or — God forbid — in the backseat of your boyfriend's little BMW convertible.

At Harkness, sexy times weren't so fraught. And although I'd had to train my roommate Scarlet to watch out for the bandanna on the doorknob of our room, the logistics were a lot easier.

For the first two months of the semester, I'd had a blast. In September, I'd dated a freshman tight end. He had an eight-pack like you read about and gorgeous, muscular thighs. But he wasn't much of a conversationalist, so I'd had to let him go. Then there was Dash, who I should probably start calling The Fullback Who Shall Not be Named. He was another freshman with lickable abs. But I broke up with him in November, because he wasn't very nice to me when we had our clothes *on*.

I'd meant to take a break from football players after that. After all, it was hockey season now. And in the spring there would be lean, muscular lacrosse players to cheer for and party with.

But then a week ago I'd run into Dash again. And I'd done something so incredibly stupid that the humiliation was going to follow me to my grave. A few stupid hours had turned me into someone who second-guessed her wardrobe, her makeup, her life choices…

My phone buzzed with a text. *Evening! I'm downstairs in your courtyard. Andy B.*

Be right down, I replied. It was sort of cute that he'd added his last initial, as if I might have forgotten who I'd invited to this little party. Andy Baschnagel was a basketball player. I didn't, as a rule, do basketball players. The sport just wasn't sexy to me. Those long baggy shorts and even longer arms? Eh. Maybe if I went to Duke or Michigan, I'd understand the appeal.

Anyway, I hadn't invited Andy B. to this party because he was a basketball player. I'd done it because he wasn't an asshole (I hoped). And because I'd pledged Tri Psi and could not show up at one of their events without a date. And for extra points, he had to be A) an athlete and B) an upperclassman. With Andy, I could check both of those boxes.

No matter that I was suddenly having trouble remembering why I cared about checking those boxes. It was too late to wonder about that now. I had a party to survive, and a guy waiting downstairs. It wasn't his fault that I would rather hide under the bed than face the people at this party. And I'd absorbed at least *some* of the ladylike manners my very proper mother had taught me.

It was time to march down there and make the best of it.

When I reached the courtyard, Andy was standing there texting someone, a smile on his face.

He looked friendly enough. And he was pretty cute for a skinny guy. But still, all that attention to his phone was not an auspicious sign. I was sick of guys who spent the whole evening texting their buddies, calculating everyone's odds of getting some action later.

"Hi," I said carefully. He still hadn't noticed me.

His head jerked up, his face guilty. "Sorry. Hi." He offered me his hand to shake. "I'm Andy."

For a second, I didn't step forward. I mean… what guy under forty shakes hands like that? Recovering myself, I took his hand, which was warm even on this cold night. "Hi. I'm Katie."

"I know," he smiled. Then he shoved his phone into his pocket even though it chimed with an incoming text.

"Don't you have to get that?" I asked. It was a little bitchy of me, honestly. But I needed to know what I was going to be dealing with.

"Nah," he said. "She can stuff it."

"Who can?" I couldn't help but ask, even as his phone rang in his pocket.

He grinned. "My sister. Sorry. Let me get rid of her." He jerked the phone out and swiped to answer. "Delia. Go dissect a cadaver or something. I'll talk to you tomorrow." There was a pause. "I love you too, even though you're bossy like Hitler. G'night."

I laughed in spite of myself. "I think you got the last word."

"It's only a temporary victory. She always wins eventually. But that's okay, because she's already doing me a big favor."

"What kind of favor?" Together we walked out of the Fresh Court gate, heading down College Street, toward Fraternity Row. I kept our pace slow, and it wasn't even because of my three-inch heels. I was dreading this party.

"Well, Delia is going to med school. Every Jewish family needs a doctor, see. And now the pressure is off me."

I laughed again. That was, like, twice in two minutes. "Really? Are your parents doctors?"

"Nope. Dad is an accountant, Mom is a librarian. But that doesn't matter. It's a cultural thing. The deli by our house even has a platter on their catering menu called the 'My Son is a Doctor' plate."

"But they won't be ordering it for you?"

"No. I might go to law school, though. That's second best."

"Interesting. My mom doesn't care what I do, just as long as I look pretty doing it." I shouldn't have said that. It was really too much sharing for the first ten minutes of a blind date.

"Well…" he cleared his throat. "At least one of us is a shoo-in for meeting the parental expectations."

My face burned a little then, because I'd made it sound like I was fishing for compliments. "That's nice of you," I said quietly. "Do you have just the one sister?"

"Nope" he said cheerfully, giving me another smile. When Andy smiled, his angular face softened up, taking him from ordinary to pretty damned attractive in one leap. It was kind of spellbinding, really. "I have another sister, too. Spent my whole life getting henpecked and waiting for the bathroom. I thought I came to Harkness to get away from them. But then I couldn't figure out why my freshman bathroom was so gross and smelly all the time."

"See, girls aren't so bad," I said.

"True dat."

We were within a hundred yards of the Tri Psi house now, and I had slowed our pace practically to a crawl.

"Do your feet hurt?" Andy asked, looking down.

That made me smile, because it was so obvious that Andy did

have sisters. "My feet are fine. I'm just having second thoughts about tonight, that's all." I stopped walking altogether.

Andy stopped too, folding his arms. "Yeah?"

"Yeah," I sighed. (Even though "yeah" sounded cheap. Sorry, Mom.)

He stood very still, studying me. "Look," he said, tugging on an ear. "Is it me? I mean, if you changed your mind…"

"What?" *Oh, hell.* I reached out to put a hand on his arm, giving it a squeeze. "Jeez, no. You are *not* the problem. This is all on me."

But he was still frowning, and his brown eyes were filled with concern. "Then what's the matter?"

"Well…" my eyes drifted toward the big white house on the corner. I'd always had fun there. But tonight I didn't want to set foot in the place. "I'm pledging the sorority. And we just spent a whole lot of hours setting up a holiday toy drive. The party for the kids is tomorrow. And tonight we're supposed to wrap the gifts, which should be fun, right?"

"Sure?"

"But the Beta Rho guys are setting up our tree on the sun porch. And I really don't feel like seeing them tonight, that's all."

"Is one of them your ex, or something?"

I let out a big old sigh. "Yes. But also his friends… There are *several* guys that I don't want to see."

Andy looked toward the house, and then down at me. "Do you mind if I ask why? I mean… are they scaring you?"

I shook my head. "It's not like that. It's just…" The moment stretched out, because there was no way I could actually tell him why. It was deeply embarrassing to me, and if he knew what I'd done, he'd stop looking at me the way he was looking at me now. His eyes were soft, and he'd given me his complete attention. He looked at me as if I were important. And I didn't want to see how that expression would change if he heard the stupid thing that I'd done.

But he was waiting for an answer. And I owed him one, because I was the idiot who had us standing out here in the cold.

"Okay," I tried. "My mother has a saying that you shouldn't do anything you don't want reported on the front page of the *New York Times*. And I've never been very good at following that rule, although

I wish I were. Because my ex and his pals weren't very nice about... a recent embarrassing episode."

Again, Andy's brown eyes darted over to the sorority house and then back. But his frown lost some of its depth. With what I'd just told him, he would probably assume that I'd gotten drunk and puked all over the place, or something. "Well, okay. Going in or not is your call. We could always just go for ice cream at Scoops instead. I saw on Facebook that they made a new batch of salted caramel today. That's my favorite flavor."

I reached across to give his arm another squeeze. "I like your style, Andy. And it's tempting. But then they win, right?"

Andy shrugged. "You could look at it that way. Or you could just say that life is too short to spend even ten minutes with assholes."

Aw. This guy! I liked him already. "You are a very smart man. But I spent a lot of time on this charity thing, and if I don't see it to completion, I'm going to feel bad about that, too. So tonight I'm going to put on my big girl panties and give it a shot."

"Fine." His face lit up then with another winning smile. "But if you change your mind, what's the word? Give me a code so I'll know when to help you bail out."

"How about 'scoop'? As in ice cream."

"Deal. If you say 'what's the scoop?' we're outie." Then he held out his arm in that formal way, as if escorting a lady to dinner inside the pages of a Jane Austen novel. That was even weirder than shaking my hand. But so what? I took his arm, and in we went.

CHAPTER 3
ANDY

TOGETHER, we climbed a set of wide steps, passing a perfect row of rocking chairs on the porch. Until tonight, I'd never been inside of a sorority house. To me, they were mythical places, where the toilet seat was always down and the air smelled of flowers instead of feet. I opened the door, then stood aside for Katie.

And then we were inside, and the place did not disappoint. Like so many of the buildings at Harkness, Tri Psi had been built about a hundred years ago. The big front room had high, beamed ceilings. On one wall rose an oversized stone fireplace, where orange flames licked the air behind an iron metal grate.

All around the room, shiny-haired girls buzzed like bees. It was just the sort of estrogen-fueled chaos that reminded me a lot of my sisters.

Katie tagged one of the girls on the elbow as she flitted by. "Amy?"

She turned to look over her shoulder, smiling at us. "Hey! You look gorgeous. And have I met your date?"

I was introduced to Amy, who seemed to be in charge. She rattled off a bunch of instructions to Katie at warp speed — there were tables to set up and rolls of paper to find and toys to wrap. Katie nodded along at this barrage of details. But when Amy moved on, Katie turned to me with a smile. "First things first." She sidled up to a table bearing a metal tub full of ice, with dozens of bottles of beer nested inside. This was obviously not a keg-and-red-plastic-cup affair.

"Thanks," I said when she handed me a cold beer. "What's next? You can put me to work." Honestly, I was thrilled that this party had a mission other than small talk or — God forbid — dancing.

In high school, I was the scrawny nerd who never got invited to parties. Even though I'd grown into my long legs and stopped getting shoved into lockers years ago, I had never mastered small talk. And we won't even *talk* about what kind of a dancer I was. Because that way lies the abyss.

College had been much more fun for me than high school. Except for my nonexistent love life, I was happy at Harkness. Although our basketball team kind of sucked, my teammates were happy to have me. And on a basketball court I always knew what to do. I knew to always be ready to catch the pass. To find an opening and go for it.

But at a party? It was like I'd never received the playbook that everyone else got at birth. A party with Katie Vickery was double trouble, because her hotness made me into more of a bumbler than usual. A job was just what I needed.

Katie shifted her weight from one long leg to the other. "Well... most of the guys will be in that room," she tilted her head toward an arched doorway at the side. "They're putting up the tree. But if you wanted to stay here with me, you could help with the wrapping."

For a second I wasn't sure what to do. I didn't want to be under-foot. But there was something hesitant in in Katie's expression. As if perhaps she could use a little backup. "I'd just as soon help you, if that's okay," I said.

I knew I'd made the right choice, because the most beautiful smile lit her face. "Awesome. Then will you help me set up a folding table? Last time, mine fell down on one end, like a wounded camel. And all the Halloween pumpkins went rolling off."

Well, okay then.

There was a stack of collapsed folding tables leaning against one wall. I grabbed one and let Katie show me where to set it up, which took about sixty seconds. Then I drank my beer while she went running off for wrapping paper and tape. The beehive was in full swing around me. There were girls on the old wooden staircase, wrapping strands of Christmas lights around the banister, and girls toting boxes of Christmas cookies through the front door.

Katie returned with three enormous rolls of wrapping paper. "I'll just grab the first stack of gifts," she said.

"Are you sure I can't help with that?" I asked.

She waved me off. "It's mayhem back there. I'll be right back." True to her word, she soon reappeared with a stack of boxes. They were rainbow looms — those things that little kids used to make bracelets out of rubber bands.

Measuring the boxes, I began cutting pieces of Santa Claus paper to size. Functioning as an assembly line, Katie and I became a wrapping machine. I cut. She folded and taped. Working side by side made it easy for me to admire Katie. As she moved, her silky hair fell over her shoulder like a curtain. It made me want to sift my fingers through it, to see if it was as soft as it looked. And the way her dress skimmed her hips was making me a little bit crazy. In a perfect world, I would have loved to fit my hands around her waist.

Down, boy. I lowered my head and cut another rectangle of wrapping paper instead.

When every box was wrapped, Katie disappeared for a minute into a closet, returning with a towering stack of… basketballs! Some of them were ordinary basketballs, and pretty good quality. Others were meant for little kids, with cartoon pictures drawn all over them.

"Now we're talking," I said. "Those are some lucky kids if they're getting these."

"Glad you think so," she said. "But they're not going to be easy to wrap."

I saw what she meant. The balls were in half-boxes, which meant that one side would cave in a bit when we taped it. "It will work," I told her. "This is just karmic payback for all those years my mother had to figure out how to wrap basketballs for me in blue and white Hanukkah paper."

Katie gave me a killer smile. Then she unrolled a long span of wrapping paper, this one in plain green. Then she grabbed a ball — there were bears on this one — and set its oddly shaped carton onto the paper.

"Hold up…" I gave her the hand signal for time-out. "We can't wrap the kiddie balls in that plain paper, unless you're putting name tags on each of these. The paper should signal what's inside, right? A guy who chooses the green wrap can't end up with Disney characters on his basketball. He's going to get his ass kicked."

Katie's hands stilled. Then she and Amy, who was wrapping stacks of teddy bears nearby, both began to laugh. "Omigod, so true!" Katie said. She swapped the ball for a plain one. "The bigger question is, did I screw this up? Should I have not bought the decorated ones at all?"

I shook my head. "Those are good for little kids, because the bigger kids won't steal them. No cool dude is going to bring a ball with pandas on it to his pickup game."

"These are all good points," Amy remarked. "And now I'm thinking that we should put age ranges on everything. We could write, 'a sporty gift for up to age six.' Would that work?" She raised her eyes to me.

"Well, sure."

While Katie's sorority sister ran off to find some paper to make the tags, Katie touched the cuff of my shirt. "You are really good at this. Thank you for helping."

I shrugged. "I had lots of experience getting my ass kicked. I know all the scenarios."

Giggling, she touched a warm hand to my back for a second as she reached for the tape. Every time she put one of those slim hands on me, I felt it everywhere. And she smelled incredible. Like strawberries. I don't know what it was — a lotion? A fruity shampoo? Whatever it was, it was making me crazy.

"I really wasn't sure what to buy for the boys," she said, leaning over the next gift. "I hope these have a shot at making someone happy. There were trendier toys at the store, like action figures. But I went with sturdier things, and I hope it was the right call. These kids don't get to make a list and choose."

I cut the next piece of wrapping paper, thinking about that. "Even when you get to choose, gift-giving is never perfect, right? I asked for a lot of stuff as a kid only to find out it wasn't as good as it looked on TV."

"Ha! That is *so* true. My EZ Chef Oven never baked the cakes all the way through. I just hope that something here makes somebody's day, you know?"

"It has to," I told her. "There's something a little magical about getting a wrapped gift, especially if it's unexpected. The experience is bigger than the thing that's inside."

She didn't answer for a second, and I didn't quite know why. But then she spoke, and her voice was quiet. "You're a smart guy, Andy B.," she said, catching another piece of tape on her slender forefinger. "And we've been here an hour, and so far I haven't had to use the secret code word."

Her eyes flicked toward the arched doorway then. The sound of male voices had been coming from that room for a while now. She didn't look happy about it.

"That offer still stands, though," I whispered.

"And I do appreciate it," she breathed.

Eventually, we got everything wrapped except for one basketball — a pink one, with ducks on it. This last ball had a torn box around it and a black ink mark on its surface. "What do we do about this one?" I asked. "Ditch the box? Tape it up?"

Katie regarded it with a frown. "This one they gave me at the store, because it's damaged and because all our purchases were for charity. But I don't think I want any kid to get a damaged gift. That's just not right."

"Without it, do you have enough toys?"

"We do."

"Fair enough." I tore the ball from its box and tossed the cardboard onto our recycling pile. Then I spun it on my fingertip. Holding a basketball — even a pink one with ducks — always made my head feel clearer.

The Christmas tree setup next door must have been almost finished, because the sound of male laughter grew louder, and guys began to wander in, beers in hand. Their new role seemed to be smirking and drinking. Katie kept her eyes glued to the gift-wrapped packages which she was busy tagging. But I noticed that her body drifted a few inches closer to me.

And I didn't mind one bit. I was flattered, honestly. If my job tonight was to provide some kind of cover, I could do that.

Now, nice guys usually got friend-zoned. That wasn't only true in movies. I was living proof. And there were days when that got depressing. But tonight I was just where I wanted to be. I didn't mind being needed by this fabulous creature. Because, what a view! And these girls had good taste in beer.

Really, things could be worse.

With her laser focus, Katie leaned over another gift tag, that silky hair cascading off her shoulder and into her work, where I saw the ends begin to adhere to the tape in its dispenser. "Hang on," I said, hooking the pale strands with my thumb. "You don't want to tape yourself to that present." Gently, I released her hair from the adhesive. And then there was nothing left to do but sweep the whole bunch of her hair back and over her shoulder, where I smoothed it down where it belonged.

Her eyes locked on mine. "Thank you," she whispered.

"No problem," I said, but my voice was thick. Because touching her had made my brain take a day trip to Atlantic City.

I gathered up a stack of wrapping paper scraps and went looking for the recycling bin.

CHAPTER 4
KATIE

SO FAR, so good.

The gift wrapping had gone even faster than I'd hoped. And Andy was good company. I didn't feel like I had to be on script with him. There was a social dance I'd learned at my mother's heel. "Ask his opinion," Mom had taught me. "A man wants someone to validate his worldview."

Even at frat parties, between games of beer pong and funnels, I'd stuck to a version of the script. Flirt and dodge. Toss the hair. I knew how to listen in a way which expressed interest without giving too much away.

It was exhausting, really. And tonight, I didn't have it in me. But it seemed not to matter. Andy's quiet companionship didn't demand anything of me. That was all for the best, because I was too freaked out by the sounds of laughter bleeding in our direction.

Some of that laughter was almost certainly directed at me.

Since the gifts were wrapped and tagged now, the next step was stacking them beside the Christmas tree in preparation for the kids' party tomorrow. But I didn't do my share, because I was putting off going into the next room. Instead, I grabbed another beer for Andy, and then planted myself right next to him. I looked up into his big brown eyes and just let him ground me. "Are you ready for the exam in European Paintings?" I asked. The test was in three days.

"Not yet," he said. "I think the baroque art is going to be the hardest to memorize," he said. "All those dark canvases. They're blending together on me."

"True," I agreed. "I'm so far behind, too. I didn't make it to the last two lectures, when he reviewed the final list of artworks. I'm probably going to memorize the wrong ones."

Andy shrugged. "I copied down the entire list in my notebook. I'll make you a copy if you want."

My heart gave a little bounce. "Could you?" This guy was going to save me *twice* this week — once from being dateless, and once from being clueless.

"No problem."

Across the room, one of the brothers stood on a chair, banging a spoon against a beer bottle. It was a beefy guy that they called Whittaker up there, looking for attention. "Ladies and not-so-gentlemen!" There was laughter all around me, but I did not laugh. Neither did Andy, actually. Even as the chuckles died down, I glanced upward, over my shoulder. He met my gaze with the world's most discreet eye roll.

"...The girls of Tri Psi ought to know that this year's tree was a three case effort. That's right. It took seventy-two beers to cut this sucker down and stand it back up on your porch."

There was another smattering of laughter, but I still wasn't feeling the love. Nothing was as light and funny as it would have been a week ago. To my new, jaded eyes, the peculiar mating ritual where a bunch of big strong boys put up a tree for the sorority princesses just hit me wrong. I mean, why couldn't we put up our own freaking tree? How hard could it be? And what were we supposed to owe these bros in exchange for their labor?

Gah. I was thinking too hard again.

"...So come on in, ladies, and let us light her up for you." He hopped off the chair and lumbered into the porch room. The sisters began to follow him.

But I did not. Because I hadn't seen Dash yet tonight, though I was sure I'd heard his rasping chuckle more than once. Rationally, I knew that I was going to have to face him down at some point. I had *seven* semesters left at Harkness. And pledging this sorority meant that I'd encounter him frequently. I needed to just get past it.

Yet something stuck my Prada heels to the floorboards. I just couldn't make myself go in there. And a full-body shiver started in my shoulders and worked its way down.

A warm hand landed lightly on my back. "Katie, are you okay?"

Yes?

No.

God.

I spun around and looked up (*way* up — he must be 6'-4") into his chocolate eyes. "I think I'd like to go outside for a minute."

He blinked once. Then, without a word, he turned toward the front door.

Like a fool, I'd run out onto the porch without my coat. So immediately I broke out in goosebumps. But the cold air felt good in my lungs. I needed to calm down. Like *right now.*

"Should I get your coat?" Andy asked. "Do you want to go?"

I shook my head. As stupid as I probably looked right now, I wasn't quite ready to bail. *Jeez.* If I let myself get this freaked out about seeing all those jerks from Beta Rho, what a long year it was going to be. "Crap," I swore. *Get it together, girl.*

"Are you going to tell me what's wrong?" As Andy said that, he draped his sport coat over my bare shoulders.

"Thanks," I stammered. "I'm not usually such a drama queen."

His eyebrows arched. "Well, maybe you have a good reason."

There was curiosity in his eyes. But it wasn't judgmental. "I don't like the way they look at me," I blurted, before I could think better of it.

"Why?"

Right. The reason was much too embarrassing for polite conversation. So instead of answering, I just looked down at my shoes.

"Let's just go, then?" he suggested. "You look a little… traumatized, actually."

That's when I let out a big sigh. Because there were people in the world who had good reason to feel traumatized. But I wasn't one of them. I hadn't been raped, or injured, or abused in any way. I'd just been stupid. Very, very stupid. "Ugh," I said. "If I leave, I'm giving him too much power."

"Maybe not," Andy challenged. "What did he do?" After asking, Andy immediately clapped a hand over his own mouth. "Sorry. It's none of my business. But you have me imagining the worst, here."

Ouch. Now a nice guy was worried about me, and I didn't even deserve it. "That's the stupid thing! Everything that went down..." *Gah!* I cringed at my unfortunate choice of words, "...between Dash and me was voluntary. I wasn't even drunk. Not very, anyway."

This explanation did not seem to appease Andy. When I looked up, his face was still full of concern. I hadn't meant to talk about this tonight, or maybe ever. And certainly not with him. And now he'd know that he was on a date with someone who was crazypants.

I took one more deep breath of cold air, which helped. A little. "Okay, I broke up with him because he didn't seem all that interested in me as a person. All he wanted to do was play video games with the brothers, but I was supposed to just hang around and watch until bedtime. Like a good little woman."

"Charming."

"I know, right? In my defense, I realized pretty quickly that he wasn't worth the effort, and I told him we were through." What I might have added was the fact that Dash didn't seem very broken up about losing me. And that should have been a big clue. But I'd missed it.

The story should have ended there. Because my instinct about him had been dead on. But it *didn't* end there. And that's why I'd been hearing a chant playing inside my head all week. And the mantra was: *Stupid... stupid... stupid...*

Andy was watching me with patient eyes, waiting for an explanation. It was silent there on the porch. And somehow I kept talking. "So, last week I went over to the Beta Rho house for a few minutes, just to drop off a bin of Christmas decorations for tonight. It was quiet there that night — the usual video games but no party." I'd been telling this part of the story to my shoes, but now I looked up to find Andy watching me. God, this was going to be embarrassing. "That night, for the first time, he made a big effort to talk to me. You know, the full court press."

Andy smiled at my basketball reference, but he didn't say a word.

"He got me a glass of wine and asked me a lot of questions about my classes, and pledging Tri Psi, and…" I rolled my eyes. "Ugh. I just sort of fell under the spell. He was so sweet and patient, telling me how much he missed me…"

"So far, so good." Andy pressed. "What went wrong?"

Yikes. I hadn't told a soul about this, not even my roommates. And tomorrow, I would probably regret telling Andy. I really didn't need even more people to know this story. But I was *angry*. And I wanted someone to *know* what pigs they were.

"Okay, he played me like a hand of poker," I sighed. "After my second glass of wine on an empty stomach, and two hours of heavy flattery, he wanted me to come upstairs with him. Fool that I am, I went." I looked down at the porch floorboards again. "He took me into one of the brothers' rooms. And we…" I cleared my throat. "We fooled around a little bit."

Andy dropped his voice. "But you didn't want to?"

He was about to get the wrong idea. "That's not it. See, I didn't mind at the time. I didn't start feeling bad about it until two days later. But that night I heard some voices in the hall. I heard a couple of the brothers laughing. But the door was shut, and I didn't think anything of it."

"Oh, *shit*," Andy whispered.

I looked up quickly, catching a wince on his face. "What?"

He closed his eyes for a long moment. And when he opened them, he said, "please tell me that this was not a hole-in-the-door situation."

My stomach dropped. Was I the only one on the planet who didn't know any better than to fall for Beta Rho's pledge ritual? Slowly, I nodded.

Andy's face sagged. "I'd always just assumed that was a myth."

"Apparently, it's not." I tried to say this with nonchalance. But I don't think I pulled it off. Because my eyes began to sting. And that was no good, because, you know, *mascara*. Carefully I pressed my fingertips against my tear ducts. "I wouldn't have even known, except that I overheard a couple of them talking about it. I was studying at one of those carrels in the stacks. Have you been up there?"

Andy nodded. There were twelve floors of books, and each floor had a row of old oak study desks with little walls attached. When you really needed to study — as opposed to picking somewhere with good people-watching — the stacks were the place to go.

"I heard these two guys carrying on, and I was going to walk over there and complain. But then I heard them say his name." I swallowed then, and my throat was thick. "So I listened. And one of them had been in the hallway that night. He was telling the other one exactly what he'd seen…" I had to stop there. Not only did I not want to speak about the details, I didn't want to think about them, either. When you're getting busy with somebody, you do not want to spend your time wondering what the expression on your face looks like when you're giving a…

God. Just shoot me.

I cleared my throat. "So, thanks to me, Dash's place in the pledge class is secure." I'd come to the end of being able to talk about this nightmare.

Andy pressed the fingertips of both hands against his brow, as if he had a sudden pain there. "He earned *pledge points* for letting the other guys *watch.*" He let out an angry noise. "That's disgusting."

When he said that, the weight of my outrage grew a tiny bit lighter. All week, I'd been carrying this embarrassing secret around. And it was awfully heavy. The sound of Andy's displeasure made me feel as if I'd just handed off a portion of my anger, letting someone else carry it for a moment instead.

"I'm still an idiot," I said, because it was true.

"No! *Shit*, no. That is the lowest of the low. That is…" Andy took a deep, slow breath and let it out again. "You know all those brochures about consent that the college passed out during the first week of school?"

"Sure." They were pretty funny, actually. My roommates and I had a few giggles reading the flyers out loud to one another. Some genius had written out a script for hookups that was supposed to guarantee that both parties had consent for every sexual act. So the bullet points read like a porn film. *Do you want me to put my hand here? Does it feel good when I do this? Can I touch you here?*

As funny as that was, it didn't really apply. "But… I, uh. I consented."

Andy shook his head. "No, you didn't. Because if you had, you wouldn't feel afraid to go in there right now." He jabbed a finger toward the door.

I had absolutely no response to that. Except that the pressure in my chest loosened another percentage point or two.

Andy didn't wait for a reaction from me, though. He was on a roll. "I mean… forget common decency. Don't any of them have *sisters?* God."

"At least there wasn't any evidence," I said quietly. "When I was eavesdropping, I actually heard the brother who wasn't there ask if there were pictures. And the other one said no, because that would make it into a code violation."

"How *thoughtful* of them to avoid violating the code," Andy spat. "Are you going to report it anyway?"

That was something I'd thought about all week. "It's not like I don't feel the urge. But as far as I can tell, they didn't break any rules, let alone laws. So it would be a waste of time. Not to mention that everyone would know how stupid I was."

Andy moved fast, then. He stepped forward to wrap his arms around me, giving me a quick, fierce hug. "You weren't stupid. Trusting, maybe. But that's supposed to be a good thing to be."

I was too shaken up to decide whether or not he was right. But I did notice that Andy gave first-rate hugs. Those long arms were good for something besides dunking basketballs, I guess. Come to think of it, he was probably only hugging me for warmth. We'd been out here awhile, and I had his jacket on. "I'm sorry to dump this on you," I said into his shoulder.

He released me, stepping back. "Sorry it *happened* to you. Want to go home? You don't owe it to him to be civil."

"But I can't avoid him for four years! And it's not just him! I don't know who was standing on the other side of that door. So I don't even know who to avoid. I'm lucky it's *not* on the front page of the *New York Times*. Mom was right."

Andy stuffed his hands into his pockets, and began pacing the porch. "She wasn't, though. I don't think your mom has thought that through."

"What do you mean?"

He stopped walking and turned to me. "We all do things that we don't want to see in a newspaper. I mean, she probably has sex with your father, right?"

"Ew."

He grinned. "Sorry, but you get my point. She doesn't want *that* pictured in the *Times*, even though there's nothing wrong with it. And you didn't do anything remotely wrong, either. At the risk of sounding very pre-law, you have a reasonable expectation of privacy if you follow a guy into his room to..." he broke off the sentence, and there was an awkward pause.

"...Put some lipstick on his dipstick?" I supplied. And then I laughed. I actually *laughed* about my nightmare. Because now that I was breathing just a little bit easier, I could see just how fricking ridiculous the whole thing was. And humiliating. But still... *funny* in a way.

God, I was probably losing my mind.

But I'd made Andy's lips twitch too with my crude description of what had happened. He was trying not to laugh now, but sometimes holding it back only makes it worse.

"Go on," I told him. "We might as well laugh about it. It's either that or crying."

He let a chuckle escape. "You want me to punch him for you? I've never won a fight in my life, but this seems like a good cause."

"Well, okay," I teased. "So long as you think a trip to jail is a good use of the rest of your night."

He grinned. "With my luck, it would be a trip to the hospital, and *then* a trip to jail. But seriously, I have two sisters. The thought of someone doing that to you makes me want to deck him."

"That's really..." I swallowed hard. "Thank you. I needed to hear someone say that. I've spent the week telling myself, 'hey, it's just sex, right? No big deal.' But I'm embarrassed. And it's not the same as if we were fooling around and somebody walked in by accident."

"Of *course* it's not the same. Intentions are everything." As he said this, I saw him shiver.

"Come on," I said suddenly. Here I'd been struggling to find a reason to go back inside the house, but there was a perfectly good one standing right in front of me. I opened the door. "You're going to freeze, and catch pneumonia, and miss our art history exam. And then I won't have anyone friendly to sit next to. So we're going back in."

"If you're ready," he said.

"I'm as ready as I'll ever be." I took Andy's cold hand in mine and pulled him inside. There was nobody in the parlor anymore. Keeping hold of Andy's hand, I tugged him through the room and into the big old sunroom.

In front of us rose a giant Christmas tree with about a million white lights on it. And now I understood why the girls put the tree in here. Those million lights were reflected in the many windowpanes which circled the room. Lifting my chin, I gazed up at it, unblinking. I'd done this ever since I was a child — I'd stare at the lit Christmas tree until my vision went slightly askew and the lights blurred before my eyes. The tree was even more beautiful when you didn't focus on each pinprick of light, but saw the whole thing at once.

"Nice," Andy whispered beside me. "The kids at your party tomorrow will love it."

"I hope so. Otherwise those three cases of our beer that the Betas drank went to waste."

My date snorted, and I squeezed his hand a little tighter.

Of course, I couldn't stare at the tree forever. Or cling to Andy. Eventually, I had to look around, and even make eye contact. And it wasn't going to get any easier if I put it off.

The brave thing to do would be to just say hello to Dash and his stupid friends, as if nothing had happened. They'd forget about the little show I'd put on eventually, right?

Gah. Okay. Deep breaths.

"Let's get you another drink," I suggested. "I know I could use one." Still clutching Andy's hand like a security blanket, I steered the two of us over to a table against the wall. I had to let him go to pop the tops off of two bottles of Moosehead Lager.

"I like this beer," Andy said, taking his. "Thanks."

I took a swig of mine. Maybe a beer or ten was the right way to go.

Tonight I couldn't exactly get wasted to dull the pain. And not because I'd worry that Andy would take advantage of me. It was just the opposite — poor Andy had already shored me up once tonight. He didn't need the trouble of escorting a drunk girl home, even if I did feel like getting numb.

Now, at close range, I heard a familiar chuckle.

Steeling myself, I turned. And there he was, a beer in hand, grinning at his pledge brothers. Dash's eyes slid in my direction. They seemed to lock on me for a nanosecond, then jump to Andy. Then, just as quickly, they slid away.

Okay, that wasn't so bad. I was just about to exhale when the guy beside Dash elbowed him, a knowing smirk on his face. Lowering his beefy head to Dash's ear, he said something which made my ex-boyfriend grin.

My pulse kicked up, and I felt hot all over. Maybe I couldn't do this after all. Maybe I should duck out of a party for the first time in my *entire freaking life*, and then transfer to another college. On another continent.

That sounded like a plan.

Turning my back, I squeezed past Andy and out through the door we'd come in not five minutes ago. I trotted across the parlor, skidding to a stop in front of the fireplace. Meanwhile, my heart bounded along inside my chest like a cartoon rabbit.

"Shit," I whispered to myself.

I heard footsteps, and a few seconds later Andy appeared at my elbow. "Forget something?" he teased. But I saw worry in his face.

Looking down into the fireplace embers, I tried to think. "They're probably laughing at me right now."

"They're not," he said. "I overheard them talking about hockey, actually."

"Figures. That's all they live for. *Games*. They made my life into one of their crude little games."

Andy made an irritated noise. "They did. And that sucks."

"He acted like a pig," I said.

"He is a pig. But what would make you feel better? An apology?"

I considered that idea. "I want him to wear a t-shirt every day for a week that reads: *I am a pig*."

Andy laughed. "You should consider law school, Katie. You'd make an interesting judge."

I looked up at him then, and his warm brown eyes were smiling at me again. "That's just the sorority girl solution, Andy. Haven't you heard the joke? How many sorority girls does it take to screw in a lightbulb?"

He cocked his head like a puppy. "How many?"

"Six. One to change the lightbulb and five to make the t-shirts."

He touched his empty beer bottle to mine. "Good one, sister. Is there a frat version of that joke?"

"Sure. It takes eleven frat boys to screw in a lightbulb. One to hold the bulb, and ten to drink enough that the room starts spinning."

He gave me the hot smile again. "You are a total hoot when you're stressed out."

"Why, thank you. I'm almost as fun when I'm not stressed out." But of course he wouldn't know that, because tonight he was keeping company with a total head case. "I have to walk back into that room. The only alternative is transferring to a school in South America. Or Europe. I hear Spain is nice this time of year."

Andy winced. "They made your visit to their house into a game, but it was a game you didn't know you were playing. And now you're supposed to go in there and be social, and pretend like it never happened. Another game."

"And not knee him in the balls, or throw up, yes."

He set his empty beer down on the mantelpiece, which is probably exactly what that space had been used for since the beginning of time. "So maybe what you need to get through the next half hour is one more game. A harmless one, though. You and I can play a game with them, only they won't know they're playing."

Now I was lost. "What game?"

"Well…" he tapped a finger on the mantel. "We'll try get each guy to say the name of an animal in conversation."

"An *animal*?"

"Sure. That's what you called him. And if you're focused on that, you won't stop to worry whether they're looking at you funny."

"Andy, they *will* be looking at me funny. Because I'm going to have to have some pretty weird conversations to get an animal name out of them."

He just grinned. "Who cares? I'll be doing it, too. For points. Whoever gets the most animals wins. And no repeats."

It was the most ridiculous idea I'd ever heard. And maybe the most brilliant. "So, this is competitive?"

"Unless you're afraid to take me on."

I giggled. "*Please*. Sorority girls are *made* for this game. I'm a Division One small talk champion. Bring it, basketball dude. And maybe I can get Dash to say the word 'pig.' Since he is one."

His eyebrows shot up. "That's a good twist, honestly. It's like a trump card. A trump animal."

"Right! If I get Dash to say 'pig,' I win automatically."

"He doesn't have, like, a pet pig that I don't know about? Am I being gamed, missy?"

I shook my head. "If either one of us can get anybody to say 'pig,' we win. So it's a little like catching the golden snitch."

"Okay. I'm in. But they have to say 'pig,' and not some similar word. Because how hard would it be to get a frat boy to talk about how much he likes bacon?"

"Good rule. Should we shake on it?"

With a smile, Andy offered me his hand. When I took it, we shook. Then he pulled me in for one more quick hug, which lasted only a fraction of a second. "Remember, 'scoop' is still the escape word."

"Oh, I remember," I told him. "But now I want to win this thing."

He gave me a gentle shove toward the porch. "Lead on, then. But you should know that I won't *let* you win. You're going to have to earn it."

"Do you always talk smack before a game?" I asked him. Now I was actually flirting with him. If you'd asked me two hours ago if I'd find the energy to flirt tonight, I would have said you were crazy.

"Basketball is at least fifty percent smack talk. The way my team plays, anyway."

He gave me one more of his killer smiles, and together we headed back in there.

CHAPTER 5
ANDY

KATIE'S STEP had a new swagger as she marched back into the party. She stopped to shed my sport coat, handing it over without a word. Then she squared her bare shoulders as if going into battle. (A really sexy battle.)

I shrugged the jacket on, then stooped to pick up the pink basketball I'd been playing with earlier. It had been abandoned in a corner. Tucking it under my arm, I followed Katie into the party, where one of the Beta Rho brothers was standing in front of the drinks table opening beers. Katie asked him to pop one open for me.

"Sure thing, cutie," he said.

"That would be *Katie*," my date corrected, her voice frosty.

"Right. Just like I said." The guy opened another bottle of beer and handed it to me.

"I like this lager," I said, holding up my bottle. "I don't think I've had it before."

"It's all right," he said with half a shrug. "I think we started buying Moosehead because our treasurer is Canadian."

"*Ah*," I said, reaching over to give Katie's elbow a meaningful squeeze. The game wasn't even a minute old, and I'd already scored a point with "moose."

Katie's eyebrows shot upward. Then she grabbed my hand and tugged me over to her side. Standing on tiptoe, she admonished me in a low voice. "That was clever, tall man, but it was low-hanging fruit. Don't get too used to winning."

I took the risk of putting a hand onto one of her deliciously bare shoulders and leaned down toward her ear. "You talk a big game, lady. But I don't see any action."

Her eyes flared then. And she stood up a little straighter and stalked toward her friend Amy, who was chatting with two fraternity brothers beside the tree.

Katie was a smart girl. She'd picked a target rich environment. I followed, dodging a few people. The party was in full swing now. All the work had stopped, and guys and girls stood around in twos and threes, drinking beer and munching Christmas cookies.

Katie's eyes were darting around the room, as if she were looking for something. But what? I'd already clocked Dash, her ex — and who calls himself "Dash" anyway? — about ten feet from Katie. Then I saw her swoop down and gather something up. When she stood up again, there was a sparkle in her eye. And a cat in her arms.

She gave me a victorious glance, then tossed all that gleaming hair over her shoulders. I maneuvered closer to her, so that I could hear whatever went down.

Katie waited for a pause in Amy's conversation with the two beefy guys before her. "Careful," Amy said, turning to Katie. "Mr. Whiskers is going to scratch your dress."

"He wouldn't dare," Katie said. "Cats like me." With an innocent face, she looked up at one of the guys in front of her. "How do you feel about cats?"

"I'm more of a dog person," he said, swigging his beer.

"Are you now?" Katie said, throwing a meaningful glance over her shoulder at me. She bent her knees to release the cat. Mr. Whiskers disappeared under the Christmas tree. Then Katie gave a big sneeze. "Excuse me a moment," she said.

I followed as Katie made a beeline for a box of tissues on a side table. "I'm allergic to cats," she said, blowing her nose. "But that was totally worth it."

"So you threw yourself on the sword for that point?"

"I did," she agreed, blowing her nose.

"Well, as Teddy Roosevelt said, 'greatness is the fruit of toil and sacrifice and high courage.'" God, I was such a dork. But Katie was still smiling, so it didn't really matter.

"I'm winning this thing," she said.

"You're *tying* this thing. The score is 1–1, smack-talker."

With a fiery look at me — one which I felt in some very inappropriate places — she marched off again.

CHAPTER 6
KATIE

THE ROOM WAS MORE crowded tonight than I'd anticipated. Everyone was taking this last opportunity to have a beer with friends before we all hunkered down for exams. As I waded back into the thick of things, I was halted by the sight of a girl's limbs wrapped around Dash.

That was fast.

Peeking through the boughs of the Christmas tree, I snuck a closer look. When the girl shifted her face from one side of him to the other, I recognized her. *Debbie Dunn.* She wore an unhealthy amount of eye makeup. And was staring up into Dash's face, and practically rubbing her boobs on his oxford shirt.

My first thought was: *Ew.* My second was: *Have I ever done that? And did it cause someone else to say 'ew'?* My third thought was: *Do I care? Am I actually* slut-shaming *Debbie Dunn because she's wearing gloppy mascara?*

My fourth thought was: *When did I start over-thinking absolutely everything? And how can I stop?*

Abruptly, I moved around the Christmas tree, looking for someone else to talk animals with. Andy had been right about one thing. It was hard to second-guess yourself to death when you were trying to come up with a reason for your neighborhood frat boy to say *hedgehog.* Or *platypus.*

For now, I steered a wide path around Dash. Later, maybe I would try to get him to say *octopus*. Because that's what Debbie reminded me of.

Gah! Catty, much? There I went again, worrying about the wrong things. Because, hell, the girl was actually doing me a *favor*. If Dash was busy allowing Debbie to slither up his body like a sea creature, he couldn't exactly make any crude comments about me (or my recent performance) to his pals.

I should thank her. I should buy her flowers. (Because Dash never would. That was for damned sure. He wasn't a fan of "romantic shit," he'd said once.)

And anyway, a few yards from where I stood, Andy was busy talking to Dash's pledge mate, the one they called Ralph. "You're from Chicago?" I heard Andy say. "How do you like your football team this year?"

Crap!

"The Bears look pretty good going into the playoffs," Ralph said.

Andy's eyes flicked over to me, and I saw a corner of his mouth turn up in satisfaction. Then, after he and Ralph exchanged a few more words, Andy actually *moonwalked* backwards a few paces, as if in victory. Now, someone as tall as he was really couldn't moonwalk without making a spectacle of himself. And I saw a few eyebrows lift in his direction. But Andy seemed not to care, and that made me smile.

Once upon a time, I'd felt that way, too. In high school, I'd found it easy to be the silly one. I had a lot of good friends, and a solid standing in the social group of my choice. And were I to have moonwalked (not that I'd ever wanted to) through a party, nobody would have cared.

Somehow I'd taken a wrong turn these past few months. I cared too much about the opinions of people who cared too little about me. That was something I was definitely going to mull over later. But right now, I had work to do. Because Andy was a point ahead of me in our weird little game.

And there was never going to be a better time to face the music. So I marched up to stand among the group of fraternity boys which included Dash, and also Whittaker.

"Evening, Katie," Whittaker said. A little smile played on his lips, making me almost certain that he'd been in on Dash's stupid little prank.

Just breathe.

"Evening, Whittaker," I said. "Are you ready for the art history exam?" He was one of Dash's football cronies in that class. I used to sit beside them every Monday, Wednesday and Friday. I'd felt smug about that, too. As if one seat in that lecture hall was better than another one. It seemed quite ridiculous now. Some other stupid girl could have that seat. Debbie, or a whole team of Debbies. I was done with it.

"Still have to memorize all those paintings," Whittaker said.

"Yeah," Andy put in. He slid in behind me and put a hand on my bare shoulder, giving it a gentle squeeze. "I'm taking that course, too. And some of those paintings are a little gruesome. You know, those Renaissance scenes? Especially that one from right after the hunt?"

Crap again! I knew where Andy was going with this. The hunt painting had a very dead wild boar in the foreground. But no way was he going to win this thing by getting Whittaker to say "boar." It had to be *pig*. No substitutions. I leaned my shoulders back against him as a silent message. *Don't think this will work for you, pal.*

He gave my shoulder another squeeze, as if to say: *don't you wish you'd thought of this?*

Whittaker scratched his head. "I don't think I know that one yet."

"Bummer," Andy said. "Add that one to your study list, then." I tipped my head back on his shoulder so I could see his face. He winked at me, and I had to bite the inside of my cheek to keep from giggling.

When I faced forward again, I found Dash watching us, and Whittaker, too. Maybe they were wondering why Andy and I kept giving each other significant glances. Or maybe they were remembering exactly how ridiculous I looked during what was supposed to be a private moment. God, I hoped it was the first thing, and not the second thing. Weirdly enough, though, I didn't care quite so much as much as I had about an hour ago.

So that's something.

"Anybody have any good plans for winter vacation?" Andy asked.

"Sailing in Fiji," Dash bragged. God, he was such a tool. I can't believe I ever thought he was a catch.

"Doing some skiing," Whittaker said.

"Yeah?" Andy perked up. "What's your favorite mountain?"

"We're heading to Utah," Whittaker answered. "Gonna hit Alta and Snowbird."

"I *love* Snowbird," Andy agreed, giving my shoulder yet another squeeze.

He would. Because now I was down by *two* points. The party would breaking up soon, too. My chance for victory would soon be over. I looked around the room, wondering how we were going to fit fifty kids in here tomorrow. "I'm glad it's not my job to set this place up in the morning. It's going to be mayhem, right?" There was another committee for that. (Sororities loved committees.) I wasn't due to help out until the party started at eleven.

Dash shrugged. "I don't think I'm going to make it over here. You girls seem to have it covered. Amy had a checklist, and shit."

The hair on the back of my neck stood up, and not because of Dash's dismissal of a party for fifty indigent children. But because I had my Hail Mary idea. "It must be really hard to plan parties," I said in a wistful tone. "I mean… where is Amy going to find all the tables and chairs that we need? Does anyone, like, deliver those things?"

I felt Andy stop breathing. Because he saw where I was going with this.

Dash gave another indifferent shrug. "She probably just called a party rental company."

"Huh," I said slowly. "Like that one with those trucks I see around campus sometimes? Those bright ones with…" *Take the bait*, I prayed. *This is for all the marbles.*

"Yeah," he drained his beer. "With the pink pigs on 'em."

Andy's hand closed firmly around my elbow, as if to say, *I can't believe you pulled that off*. And I gave him a subtle bump with my hip. *Take that, tall guy*. I felt rather than saw the smile that he ducked his head to conceal. When he let out a nearly silent chuff of laughter, his nose grazed my hair, and his breath at the back of my neck gave me goose bumps. In a good way.

And through it all, Dash just stood there in front of me, looking half bored and half uncomfortable, worrying the label on his beer bottle. And then Debbie slithered up to him again, plastering herself against his side. She shot me an ornery look.

"Welp!" I said, turning toward Andy. "I think I'm done here. After I duck into the ladies' room, do you mind if we head out?"

"Not at all," he said, spinning the pink basketball on one finger.

"Back in a jiff," I promised. I crossed the room, which was already beginning to thin out. It was still early, but exam week wasn't the best time to party, even for this crew. And tomorrow the sorority was hosting fifty kids. A hangover would not be welcome in the morning.

I crossed through the parlor to the big old bathroom. Like so many buildings at Harkness, it was a blend of old-world grandeur (the marble tiles) and awkward 1970s renovations (the creaky metal doors on the toilets).

After I took care of business, I emerged from the stall to find Debbie in front of the single tiny mirror, refreshing her lipstick. Washing my hands, I began to feel philosophical. "That spot where you're standing," I said to Debbie, "is where we usually have elbow-jousting matches. Primping is practically a blood sport around here."

"If I had your face, I wouldn't bother primping," Debbie said in a low voice.

I stared down at the paper towel in my hands. On the one hand, I really didn't understand why she'd say that. But we girls put ourselves down often enough, even if we don't usually do it for people who aren't already our friends. I didn't know what to say.

But while I struggled to figure it out, Debbie spoke again. "I don't know why he broke up with you, either. If you lasted a month, I'll probably last a week."

"Whoa. Hey now," I said, hands on my hips. "Don't you dare give him all that power. Maybe he doesn't get to decide."

She gave me a sullen glance. "Of course he does. They already have the power."

"Debbie."

She turned to me, her eyes dark.

"He isn't worth it, okay? Go out with him if you want. Or not. But treat yourself right. Because he's not going to look out for you."

She gave me a little eye roll. "Everybody gets dumped, Katie. Even you."

"But I didn't. I broke up with him."

"Sure you did," she said immediately. Her words had dismissed me, but her eyes were interested.

"I did. And then he decided to teach me a little lesson."

"How?" she whispered, unable to hide her curiosity.

"I was stupid. I fooled around with him one more time…" God, I didn't want to say this next part out loud. But she deserved to know what she was getting herself into. "Without my knowledge, he let some people watch."

Her eyebrows shot straight up, disappearing into her bangs. "Like, through a hole in the door?"

Kill me now. I really was the only naive idiot left on this campus, wasn't I? Slowly, I nodded.

"That is so wrong," she hissed.

"You think?"

She stuffed makeup products back into her clutch purse. "You know, fuck it. I'm just going to sneak out and go home. He's been giving me a not-so-nice vibe all night. And that is just too much." She jammed the bag under her arm. "Good night."

Without another word, she stormed out of the bathroom.

Then it was just me alone with the little mirror. And I felt an instinctual pull to go over to it and check my makeup. Because you never know when your eyeliner has smeared…

No, I coached myself. *Andy's waiting. And he doesn't care about your stupid makeup.*

I pushed open the bathroom door and went to find him.

CHAPTER 7
ANDY

WHEN KATIE DEPARTED for the bathroom, it left me standing there with Dash and his thick-necked pals. I'd had enough to drink. So instead of reaching for another beer, I began to noodle around with the outrageous pink basketball I'd been carrying around. I rolled it up the back of my hand and along my arm. Then I dribbled it a couple of times on the old wooden floor beneath me.

"Nice ball you've got there," Dash muttered. "Is your team switching *teams* this season?"

A gay joke from a frat guy? *Shocker.* "You know, it's not nice to make fun of a guy's balls," I quipped. Nothing he could say right now could ruin my mood. I still wouldn't have minded landing a punch right in the middle of his smirk. But I wasn't going to do it. Because fighting Dash and his crew was a pretty bad idea, one which would surely mess up the plan I had to walk Katie home and ask her out.

Eyes on the prize, and all.

Ignoring Dash, I toyed with the ball, spinning it on my finger and dribbling through my legs. This always relaxed me. Whenever I was stressed out about something, I took the ball in my hands and began to calm down.

Still, I could feel him watching me. Maybe he thought I was showing off, but it wasn't really like that. If I wanted to show off, I'd do these tricks twice as fast. I was just taking things nice and easy, letting the ball slide off my palms, feeling the satisfying bounce of rubber against wood and then skin.

"Pass," Dash said.

Really, dude? You have to get competitive? Maybe he didn't enjoy the fact that I was friendly with his ex-girlfriend. What a tool.

I passed him the ball. He palmed it, then bent his knees to execute a couple behind-the-back bounces. Then once under the knee. And then he bounced it back to me.

You want to show off? Fine. For the next fifteen seconds, I gave it to him: bang-bang under one leg, followed by a scissor cross, a few strokes of walking the dog, and then a quick bounce back to him.

He fumbled it, which made me irrationally happy. Then he did a little handiwork with a triangle dribble around his right leg (and I'd bet money he couldn't do his left) before a fake and a snap back to me.

The fake and the snap were exactly what I thought he'd do. So I took that ball as if I'd been waiting for it all my life. Slowing it down, I dribbled around my body a few times, spinning it on a fingertip after that. "Stay ready," I warned him.

He lifted a brow, irritated that I'd warn him like that. As if he were a bumbler. (Even if he was.)

I dropped the ball low in front of me, pounding the dribble for four or five strokes. Then I let go. The ball ricocheted up… and *straight* into Dash's crotch.

Three-pointer! So to speak.

"URMMFFF!" the guy groaned, catching the ball and bending over in the time-honored position of a guy whose eggs had just been scrambled.

It took all my effort not to laugh. "Ouch," I said.

"You *ass*," Dash muttered. And when he straightened up, his face was red with anger.

My heart rate kicked up a couple of points, but I held his gaze. "That hurts, right? When you think you've signed up for a simple game of one-on-one, but then it turns out that someone else had different plans for you?"

His face did something interesting then. It locked up tight in surprise. And then guilt crossed his features. His mouth sagged, and his eyes looked away from me. He swallowed uncomfortably.

"You can call me an ass if it makes you feel better," I said in a low voice. "But you leave Katie alone."

Dash didn't acknowledge me. He just set the ridiculous pink basketball down on a wicker chair, and then picked up a sport coat that had been lying over the back of it.

"You get me?" I pressed. That's when I heard the sound of high heels tapping toward me. "Hey!" Katie said, skidding up to me. "Sorry about that. I got caught up chatting in the bathroom."

"No problem." I turned to give her my full attention and was basically walloped all over again by how attractive she was. Her silky hair slid over her bare shoulders as she moved. And those kissable lips gave me a little smile. "Are you ready to head out?" I asked, hoping the answer was yes.

"Sure! We can grab my coat on the way."

A frat brother nudged Dash, whose face was still red and ornery. "Let's hit it, bro," he said.

Dash cleared his throat. "I was waiting for Debbie. She might still be in the bathroom."

Katie paused, her hand grabbing mine. "She left," she told Dash.

"What?"

Katie's grin took on a devilish glint. "She said she had more important places to be. Or something like that. G'night." She gave my hand a little tug, and we left the room together.

PART TWO

CHAPTER 8
ANDY

WHEN KATIE HAD PUT her coat on, she'd had to drop my hand. Now that we were walking along the sidewalk together, I wanted it back. *Your only real problem is confidence*, my sister had said. What would a confident guy do in this situation?

As casually as I could, I reached over and took Katie's smooth hand in mine. She laced her fingers in mine, just like that.

Huh. *Thank you, Delia.*

"Your game saved me tonight," Katie said. "But what on earth inspired it?"

"Ah," I said, as my thumb skimmed her palm. "During the summer, I work at a boys' sleep-away camp in the White Mountains. And we're always having to think up games to keep them from fighting with each other before dinnertime."

"So you *counseled* me, like one of your nine-year-old campers?" She was smiling again, which I loved.

"Well, they're twelve. But, yeah." Maybe I was a sap, but tonight I felt truly connected to someone for the first time in a long while. Katie might not remember this night except as a blip on her way toward feeling better about the shitty thing that happened to her. But I wasn't going to forget it any time soon.

"So, you know my tale of woe," she said. "What's your story? No girlfriend, I guess?"

"Not at the moment," I said, because it sounded smoother than *my dry spell is as vast as the Sahara.* "I've dated two girls at Harkness. One my frosh year, and one last year. But, um…" I chuckled, because my tale of woe was more funny than sad. "Turns out I wasn't a good match for either girl."

"Bad breakups?" she guessed.

"Nope. I'm still friends with both of them, actually."

"But you got your heart broken?"

"Not exactly. There wasn't a whole lot of spark there in the first place. That was the problem. Both of my ex-girlfriends decided — right after dating me — that they would rather be with women."

I watched Katie's face as she took that in, waiting for the inevitable reaction. Her eyes flicked toward mine, and she bit her lip, trying to fight off her amusement. Those pretty eyes were sparkling now. "Go ahead," I told her. "You can laugh. Everyone else does."

"Oh, Andy," she giggled. "Both of them?"

"Yep."

Her giggle became an unruly belly laugh, and we had to stop on the sidewalk while she pulled herself together. She took a deep, gasping breath and wiped her eyes. "You know that had nothing to do with you, right?" she said eventually. "You didn't turn those girls gay."

"Yeah, I know it. But my friends are pretty amused anyway."

"*Both* girls," she tittered.

"Yep!"

We had almost arrived at Fresh Court, and the inevitable end of the night. This was the moment when I had to screw up my courage and ask her if we could go out again some time. But how to phrase it? Some guys were smooth and could ask for anything.

I was not one of them.

"Wait." Katie tugged on my hand just as we were about to walk underneath the Fresh Court gate. "Are you going to copy the art history notes for me?"

I paused. Did she mean tonight? "Any time. My printer makes copies."

"Can I get them now? The test is only three days away."

"Well, sure." I changed direction, steering us toward Beaumont. Katie's fingers gave mine a squeeze, which I returned. That little exchange made me ridiculously, irrationally happy. I walked on, as if it were the most ordinary thing in the world to have Katie Vickery stop by my room. But inside, I was dancing a jig.

Calm down, idiot, I chided myself. *The girl is just very serious about her art history exam.*

Even at the pace of someone walking on high heels, the trip from the gate to my entryway only took a few minutes. But that was plenty of time to fret about the condition of my room. For once I'd made the bed. *Yes!* I'd straightened it out, anyway, because I needed a surface on which to lay the evidence of my not-very-masculine fashion crisis.

Wait — I'd picked all those clothes up afterwards, right?

Uh, oh. This was going to be bad.

But it was too late to worry, because we were already arriving at my entryway stairs. Katie followed me up to the second floor, where I unlocked the door. Peering into the room, I gave a split second prayer that either things weren't as bad as I remembered, or else elves had come by to tidy up while I was gone.

No such luck. The bed was covered with my clothes. Stepping into my room behind me, my date laughed. "Looks just like my room."

"I was in kind of a hurry," I said, lamely.

"See? That's what I tell Scarlet when she complains about the mess. But apparently I'm *always* in a hurry."

Embarrassed, I went over to the desk to find my History of Art notebook. Flipping through the pages, I said, "The review lecture took me six pages. But it will only take a couple of minutes to copy."

"No rush," she said, sitting down in my desk chair, which was mercifully clean.

No rush, my brain repeated, listening for clues.

Stop, I ordered myself. Don't fuck this up. Give the girl her notes, walk her home, ask her out and count your blessings.

CHAPTER 9
KATIE

I WATCHED Andy fumble with his printer. While it warmed up, he moved over to the bed and grabbed an armload of clothes. Most of them were shirts, still on their hangers. These he ferried to the closet, jamming them onto the bar and shutting the door. If another guy did that, I would assume that he was trying to clear off the bed, in order to steer me onto it. But Andy didn't give off that hey-baby-come-upstairs-to-see-my-trophies vibe. And it was refreshing. I was so *done* with guys who had big expectations and very little gratitude.

In contrast, Andy reminded me a bit of a chocolate lab puppy — cute and clumsy. He even had big puppy feet.

As I watched him frowning over his art history notebook, I found myself wondering what it would be like to kiss him. Tonight it had dawned on me that I'd approached the dating scene at Harkness all wrong. Someone like Andy, who didn't carry himself like God's natural gift to women, probably had a whole lot of untapped passion.

Now, conventional wisdom said that confidence was a turn-on. And that was true, but only up to a point. Because confidence implied experience. And I was learning that experience wasn't all it was cracked up to be. Both my football players had plenty of experience. But neither one had ever made me feel as if our moments together were truly special.

Except for that last night with Dash. That was the only time he ever convinced me that I made a difference. And that had turned out to be a big fat lie.

Ugh.

It's just sex, I reminded myself. But I liked sex, and I'd often enjoyed it with him. Both of my football players had had beautiful bodies and plentiful stamina. In fact, if someone had asked me to draw a picture of the kind of guy I thought I wanted, I would have ended up with a likeness of them.

But it hadn't been enough, had it?

Andy handed me the first page of notes, still warm from the printer. "Have a look at this, and tell me if any of the handwriting is inscrutable," he said.

I scanned the page. Each painting's title was listed carefully, along with its artist, approximate date of creation, and sometimes the materials used.

He leaned over my shoulder, and for a weird moment I wondered if he was looking down my dress. And I kind of hoped he was. Judge me if you will.

But no. His long fingers touched the page in front of me. "Wherever I didn't write down the materials, that's because it was oil on canvas," he said. "There are a lot of those. And I may have misspelled Caravaggio. That's kind of embarrassing."

"No, that's right," I said. "One R and two Gs."

He flashed me a smile that said "friendly" more than it said "do me." Then he went over to flip the notebook around in the printer. "Good thing."

When I received the second sheet, I found a little drawing in the corner. "What's this?"

Andy sat down on the bed and folded his long arms onto his knees. "That is an X-wing fighter. Don't judge."

Aw. "I would never!"

His warm brown eyes smiled back at me again. "Good. Because there may be some rebel ships on the next page. I had to amuse myself while that blowhard in the Knicks hat asked seventeen questions."

I knew exactly which student he meant. And the guy really was a blowhard. But I teased Andy anyway. "Now, now. Do you hate him because he always wants to talk about Cubism? Or because he wears a Knicks hat?"

Andy gave me a full-on smile this time, and it was really pretty hot. "Both."

"Who's your team?" Not for nothing had I learned how to talk sports, even when I didn't give a damn. But boys? They loved it.

"I'm a Celtics fan. Not that it's easy."

"They're not a good team?"

He put a hand to his chest in mock distress. "Katie, they're the best team. It's just that they lose most of the time."

"How is that possible?"

Andy blinked at me with wide eyes. Then he leaned over the printer to copy the last two pages of notes. "Aren't we surrounded by evidence that the people who win are not always deserving?"

Interesting. I was pretty sure he wasn't talking about basketball anymore. "Thanks for your notes," I said softly. "It's going to make a huge difference."

"Don't mention it." He stapled the sheets together and handed them to me. And that was the moment when I no longer had a reason to stay there, chatting with the nicest guy I'd met in forever.

We'd reached that moment. The one which concluded the predictable chapter of our evening. Now a page would be turned. And we might find "THE END" stamped there. But I found that I wasn't really ready to hear those words. I'd taken a big gamble telling Andy my uncomfortable little story. And trusting him with it had been the smartest thing I'd done all week. He'd let me get mad, and he didn't think I was an idiot. I'd know it if he did. Those big eyes were just too expressive to hide it.

I wanted a little more of Andy. Truly I did. I stood up, then, and turned to him.

Unfortunately, he didn't catch the look of intent I was trying to give him. "I'll walk you back," he said quickly. He grabbed his jacket and shrugged it on.

Andy was truly adorable. And lovably uncalculating. Even *gentlemanly*. (Look, Mom! I found one.) But that would simply not do.

Not at all.

CHAPTER 10
ANDY

KATIE MOVED SLOWLY over to the door of my room, but she didn't open it. "Thank you for the notes. And for taking me to that wacky party. And for inventing a game that distracted me from feeling like a moron."

I smiled at her. In fact, I'd been grinning like a mental patient all night, probably. But she had that effect on me. "You're welcome. For all of it. Best sorority party I've ever been to."

She gave me a teasing eye roll. "Very funny. You told me earlier that it was the *only* sorority party you'd ever been to."

"That doesn't mean it's not true."

For a second, I got lost in the happy look on her face. Also, I expected her to move away from the door. But she didn't. Katie put her back against the door instead. Raising her chin, she looked up at me with soft eyes.

Hold up. Those weren't just soft eyes. They were eyes that asked for something.

Whoa. Time out.

I'd heard Bridger use the phrase "fuck me eyes," before. But it was a safe bet that I wasn't getting "fuck me eyes" from anyone. Like, *ever.* And I wouldn't know them even if I saw them. These, however, seemed to be "kiss me eyes."

I was pretty sure, anyway.

Oh, hell.

A couple more precious seconds were wasted while I did the math one more time, just to be confident I wasn't about to make a terrible mistake. *Girl steps in front of door, so you can't leave without pushing her out of the way. Girl stops, head against your door, mouth tilted up toward yours...*

Okay. Not too many ways to read that.

I stepped closer. Then, stalling, I lifted a hand to smooth that silky hair away from her face. She leaned into my hand slightly, and that tiny gesture gave me the courage to tip my face down to hers. Even then, I almost chickened out. I'd wanted to kiss this girl since the first time I saw her. This couldn't possibly be happening.

But it was.

Our lips met softly. My heart was a freight train in my chest, urging me on. But I fought the impulse to rush. Because Katie deserved better than that. I kissed her slowly. Teasingly, even. Once. Twice.

It was glorious.

She made a sweet little noise of approval, and the sound shot through me like a sonic boom. Feeling bold, I deepened the kiss. I scooped one hand into the silky hair at the back of her neck. And when she opened for me, the first slow slide of my tongue against hers sent my brain on a week-long sailing trip around the Caribbean.

Leaning in, I lost myself in Katie's sweet mouth. She tasted like wine and honey. Her hands slipped around to my back, and I practically died of happiness.

Still, after the most amazing ninety seconds of my life, I made myself pull back. Because all my blood had departed the thinking regions of my body to run south. And I needed my brain to come back online, before I somehow found a way to wreck this perfect evening. "Katie," I said, my forehead resting against hers. "Thank you for this awesome night. You are excellent company. I hope we can do it again sometime."

God, I hoped that was the right thing to say.

She was quiet for a moment. "Andy?"

"Yeah?" I whispered, my voice thick.

"Can we do it again right now?"

CHAPTER 11
KATIE

I SAW ANDY TAKE A LONG, slow blink. For a second there, he looked like he was trying to remember a formula for his physics exam. But then he gave me the cutest smile. And there was more warmth in his face right then than I'd *ever* seen in my jerkface ex's expression. For a moment I worried that he was going to be a gentleman and beg off. But once again, Andy proved that he wasn't a stupid man. His hands came up to cup my jaw, and then his mouth slanted over mine again.

This time, his kiss was filled with the most delicious tension. There was plenty of hunger in that kiss. When our tongues met, he made an achy little sound. But wrapped around his obvious need was a sweet layer of restraint. He wanted this. I could taste how much. But he wasn't going to lunge at me. He did not grab me or press me against the door.

That left us taking kiss after long, slow kiss. Each one felt a little harder to control than the last. The big hands which were so gently cradling my jaw were actually trembling.

Hottest. Thing. Ever.

If I'd been a good girl, like my mother had hoped, I wouldn't have taken this as a challenge.

I was not, however, a good girl.

I reached for him again, my palms grazing his ribs, venturing down to his waist. The feel of all that solid boy flesh under my hands was divine. He wasn't bulky like The Fullback Who Shall Not Be Named. Instead, he was taut and firm in all the right places. And as I explored his upper body, his breathing kicked up a couple of notches.

Because I've never been good about backing off, I reached around, cupping his ass. With a tug, I pulled him against me. And gabardine doesn't hide much. His belt buckle was not the only thing suddenly stabbing me in the belly.

The feel of him just lit me up. This smart, kind boy knew all the dumbest things about me. He'd received my ugliest secret without judgment. And now I was kissing the stuffing right out of him.

And he was really into it.

He broke our kiss with a groan. His lips wandered down my jaw next, and onto my neck, dropping kisses in their wake. When he moved, the part of him which was currently straining inside his pants brushed against the silk of my dress. And the result was a single and wholly unsatisfying drag of friction between my legs.

I didn't bother to hold back my moan of frustration.

At the sound of it, Andy's lips ceased their travel down my neck, and his body went completely still. Carefully, he rose up to his full height again, pulling me into a gentle hug against his chest. Into my ear, he whispered, "Katie, you are making me completely crazy. That's why I think it's time to walk you home."

In the silence which followed, I could hear only two beating hearts. "Just tell me this," I said finally. "Do you really want me to go home?"

He gave a strangled chuckle. "What I want is for you to wake up tomorrow and say, 'I had an unexpectedly great time last night. In fact, I want to see that skinny guy again.'"

"Unexpectedly great?" I whispered.

"Well, yeah. Or good. I could work with good, too."

I smiled into his neck. "Mmm." I had no trouble thinking up a few things that would feel unexpectedly great. His skin against my skin, for example. Sex had just always made sense to me. I treasured that communion, whether it was slow and sweet, or hot and wild.

The guys I'd dated weren't really fond of showing much emotion. So getting them naked had always been my go-to method for getting a glimpse of their unguarded selves. Andy wasn't like the others, though. He didn't mind sharing how he felt. But that only made me hungrier for him. All evening he'd been funny and generous. Without clothes, I imagined more of the same. Only much more intense.

That sounded *delicious*.

Still… I felt myself hesitate, and it wasn't a sensation that I was used to. Perhaps second-guessing myself was going to be a new habit. I nuzzled into his collar, where I could feel Andy's pulse ticking against my nose. I took a deep breath. He smelled like clean laundry and strong, steady boy. At that moment, I could swear that I'd known him for years.

"See," I said to his collarbone. "The last time I did something impulsive with a guy, it was a total disaster. I've spent the last week telling myself that I'm a big idiot."

His arms tightened protectively around me then, and I loved him for it.

"But I don't want to be embarrassed anymore. And I don't want to feel guilty about wanting you right now."

He took a deep, slow breath, and then let it out the same way. "I want you, too. But I'm willing to wait."

"I know." It came out as a husky whisper. "But that's why you don't have to." Reaching up, I undid the first button on his shirt. Teasing the collar apart, I stood on my tiptoes and began kissing his neck. This brought my body closer to his, and I did not waste the chance to brush against the bulge in his trousers.

Andy let out a groan that could probably be heard the next town over.

Suddenly we were lip-locked again, and simultaneously stumbling out of our shoes. Without my heels on, I was a lot shorter than him. Andy had to lean down fairly far to kiss me. So I gave him a little shove toward the bed. He took a couple of awkward steps back, until the bed collided with his legs.

Down he went, bringing me with him. Reacting fast, he tucked my head under his chin as we landed with a mutual "oof."

"Are you okay?" he laughed.

Scrambling into his lap, I said, "Yes." *Kiss*. "I." *Kiss* "Am. And I'd be even better if we could lose some of these clothes."

Andy's eyes squeezed shut. "That's… um…"

Uh oh. "Don't you want to?" I whispered. A little wave of insecurity splashed over me then. Although Andy had the flushed, lusty look of a turned-on guy. And I loved that look. The face that said: *You have my complete and undivided attention.* So I didn't really know why he'd hesitate.

He flopped backward on the bed. Instead of looking me in the eye, he pinched the bridge of his nose. "I just spent the evening hoping you could recover your appreciation for the male species. So it seems wrong to pounce on you the minute you're feeling okay again."

I leaned onto one elbow, looking down on him at close range. "The male *gender*. You are not a different species," I teased him. "Even if you all act like it sometimes."

But he did not smile. "Sorry," he murmured. "Not thinking too straight right now. I just don't want you to hate me tomorrow. Because it wouldn't be worth it." He reached for one of my hands, taking it between his two, kissing my palm.

I admired his long fingers. There was affection in his touch. I'd been basking in it all evening, whether I'd realized it or not. "I'm never hating you tomorrow," I told him.

In answer, he pulled me closer, until my head came to rest on his chest. His long fingers skimmed my hair. I had only an oblique view of his face, and he seemed to be thinking hard. Maybe too hard.

"You said something tonight about receiving a gift," I prompted him. "That there was something a little magic about receiving something from another person. That it was bigger than the thing itself."

He chuckled. "Sounds like something I might say to a pretty girl I was trying to impress."

I picked my head up. "I think it worked. And if I tell you one more time that you're thinking too much, will you believe me?" I hiked myself up farther onto his chest, looking down into his face. And then I waited to hear his answer.

CHAPTER 12
ANDY

I OPENED my eyes and looked up into Katie's stunning face. Her smile wasn't naughty like it had been before. It was happy. Somehow, on this bonkers night, I'd made her happy. And no matter what happened next, that felt like a big victory. I tugged her head back down on my chest. Her silky hair brushed my chin, and her sweet, fruity scent was doing a number on my self-control. "I've been told that before," I said.

"What?"

"That I think too much."

"There are worse complaints."

"Mmm," I said, kissing the top of her head. We were basically living out part of my fantasy life right now. Katie Vickery was lying *on my bed*. My desk lamp cast a yellow glow onto the wood paneling. From where I lay, it felt as if we were the only two people in the world. Seriously, Katie lying in my bed didn't make sense under any other construction of reality.

She sat up a little bit and finished unbuttoning my shirt. Then she kissed my neck, just below my ear. "You know better than to argue with a girl who's undressing you, right?"

"Yep," I said immediately. Because I am not an idiot. Ask anyone. I was going to let this happen. Because if I didn't, I'd regret it for the rest of my life. And everyone in this bed was there willingly, and nobody was drunk. Check and check.

"This dark blue is a great color for you, by the way."

"Thanks." *And thank you, Delia*. I grinned, wondering what I would find to say when she called tomorrow to ask how my date went.

"…And your smile is hot," Katie said, finishing the buttons.

"Your *everything* is hot," I said, sitting up. I ditched the shirt. And what the hell. I ditched the t-shirt beneath it, too.

Katie's eyes flared. And then she lowered her head, and began kissing all the recently exposed skin that she could reach.

"Arrraaahhhrrrgh," I gasped. Because I'm sexy like that. And because she'd begun working open my belt. And just the *proximity* of her hands to my groin had me throbbing.

I reached for her, finally allowing myself to run my fingers down the sides of her satiny dress, past her waist, which fit entirely into my two hands. I stopped when her hips slid into my grip. *Yesss*. She felt amazing. And then she yanked on my pants, and my boxers, too. I lifted my hips and let it all fall away.

Oh hell, pinch me. I was *naked with Katie Vickery*. Except for my dress socks. Because dress socks looked great on a naked guy.

Fail.

Quickly, I ditched my socks, and then wrapped Katie into a kiss that was probably going to last until New Year's. And then she wrapped her hand… *Oh, God*. Okay. Nothing was going to last until New Year's. Or even five minutes, unless I got a hold of myself.

So I shifted away from her ambitious fingers and carefully lifted her dress over her head. But that only made me hotter. Because now I had a full-on view of the sexiest bra that had ever made an appearance in my (real) life. It was lacy and black, and my eyes were probably bugging out just looking at it.

Katie wiggled out of a pair of stockings, revealing the smallest lace panties ever manufactured. Seriously, the physics lab up on Science Hill could attempt to split them like an atom in the particle accelerator.

I think I stopped breathing.

My brain took a sabbatical to Tahiti.

CHAPTER 13
KATIE

OKAY, who knew I'd become a basketball fan tonight?

After his big hands scooped my dress up over my head, Andy stretched, elongating that powerful torso as he reached over his head. I was almost too busy drooling over his tight chest to notice that he'd taken care to lay my dress over the chair.

I reclined on the bed, and Andy propped himself up on his elbows over my body. Dropping his head, he began to trace the outline of my strapless it-fits-under-every-dress bra with his tongue.

My modest cleavage had never been my best attribute. But as he kissed me, Andy made the kind of low, happy noise of a man who had just been given exactly what he craved. And as if that wasn't sexy enough, he raised his eyes to mine, his expression burning hot. I didn't know if he was asking for permission or merely trying to torture me. But I'd never felt quite like the center of someone's universe before. The slow slide of his lips coupled with that heated gaze had me tingling. Everywhere.

His lips skimmed lower, and then lower still. He began dropping soft, open-mouthed kisses just at the top of my panties. He lifted those eyes again, and the coal-dark stare was back, its intensity redoubled. I began to practically squirm with desire. In a second, I was probably going to start begging. At last, he dropped his mouth onto the lace between my legs and kissed me gently. All without breaking eye contact.

I was almost too turned on to care that there was only enough friction to make promises, not to deliver. The sight of his lean, muscular shoulders and biceps framing my legs was something I won't soon forget. I panted while he teased me with the barest touch. And when he pressed his lips against my body and groaned, I thought I would *die*.

Okay, enough with the teasing.

I plunged my fingers into his hair, then gave his head a little tug. He came willingly, all that firm skin and muscle covering me like I wanted it to. And then we were kissing again, so deeply that I tasted more of Andy than of myself.

The heavy beat of a dance tune began to pulse on the other side of Andy's wall. For a second I was under the illusion that the sound was my own heartbeat, amplified. Because I was throbbing. *Everywhere.* And then — hallelujah — he hooked the bikini strap of my panties with one thumb and dragged them down.

We made out with incredible urgency, as if a meteor were about to obliterate the earth. Our two bodies moved together, the hot beat of his neighbor's music urging us on.

"Katie," Andy breathed between kisses. "Should I find a…"

I gave him one more hard kiss, and then a shove on the shoulder to encourage him. "Go. Hurry."

He was up like a shot and rifling through his top dresser drawer. But after ten seconds of fervent scraping around, I began to get nervous. It was all well and good to be with the sweet sort of guy who didn't expect you to put out. But when push was ready to come to shove, having the necessary equipment was awfully important.

Luckily, he found what he was looking for.

A half second later, Andy was back on the bed and sheathing himself with hands so eager that they shook. I saw him take a deep breath and gather himself together. Instead of climbing on top of me, though, he gave me a little nudge and lay down beside me, pulling me into his arms. He inhaled deeply again and let it out slowly.

I trailed my hand down his chest. "Second thoughts?" I asked, hoping he wouldn't say yes.

He shook his head. "No way. You?"

"Not a chance." But even as I said it, I had the first quiver of uncertainty I'd ever experienced just before sex. A little voice in my head said: *Really, Katie? Shouldn't you feel shame for this? Other girls would.*

This stopped me for perhaps two seconds.

Oh, *shut up!* I ordered that voice. Those other girls didn't know what they were missing. I was not going to let The Football Player Who Shall Not Be Named ruin this moment for me.

Andy shifted into position over me again. But he didn't make it happen yet. Instead, he lifted his long hand to cup my face, and he kissed my forehead tenderly. "I've had a thing for you since the first art history lecture," he said.

"What?" With all his warm skin over me, it was hard to track any conversation.

"You sat in front of me with a friend," he whispered, kissing my nose. "You told her you'd always wanted to visit the Louvre and the Prado. But you were happy to take the course first. You were wearing a pink t-shirt and a denim skirt. Your friend was looking at Facebook for the whole lecture. But not you. You took notes. Your hair was held back in a pink scrunchie, and I wanted to pull that out and let your hair fall down loose."

Somewhere in the middle of that little speech I'd stopped breathing. "Wow," I gasped. I was blown away. Gone.

Above me, Andy just smiled. "But no pressure, right?"

Looking up at him, I giggled suddenly. And all the tensions of the evening fizzed up, shaking my stomach with laughter. For a second I thought that I was going to totally lose it, the way that laughter sometimes grabs a hold of you and won't let go. It was entirely possible that I was about to become hysterical.

But Andy just smiled wider. Then he lowered his grin to my jaw and kissed me there. And then he kissed the sensitive spot under my ear. And my neck. And my collarbone.

The laughter died in my throat, and I relaxed onto the bed.

"Is this okay?" he whispered, bringing his body close to mine.

"Yesss…" I breathed.

As he fitted us together, Andy groaned like a man in pain. But he moved like a man in love.

I wrapped my arms around him, drinking in his kisses.

"Katie…" he whispered, his breath catching. And the sound of it was the same sound you'd make if you'd just unwrapped an unexpected gift and found just what you'd wanted inside.

CHAPTER 14
ANDY

OH JESUS. Pinch me. Seriously.

This couldn't really be happening. Not to me. In fact, any minute now I was going to wake up in some library somewhere, face down in a puddle of my own drool. With my physics notes pasted to my face. And when they peeled off, I'd have equations tattooed all over my cheek in blue ink.

A good dream was the only plausible explanation for this moment.

And *why the fuck* was I thinking about physics notes right now? I needed to memorize this moment. Because if it was really happening, then the world was probably ending. Maybe there was a rip in the space-time continuum. Which meant that the polarity of the earth was in jeopardy. And… um…

Ohhh…

Wow.

Ohhh…

Wow.

Jeez…

Wow.

This.

This is…

So much wow.

CHAPTER 15
KATIE

Beautiful creature
A single bead of sweat at your neck
Your agonized huff of breath
As you try to hold yourself back

We have brought each other here
To this place of slicked skin against skin
Torturing each other so perfectly

"More," I beg you, because I can't help myself
And you close your eyes with gratitude
For this pretty moment

CHAPTER 16
ANDY

OH.

Oh yeah. Oh boy.

Yesyesyesyesyes.

More? Rawr…

Wow. Good. Too good. Red zone, here.

DANGER.

Quick! Picture Mrs. Dunlop's neck. Warty 5th grade teacher to the rescue!

Okay. I've got this. Except… Oh my God. Oh… wow. Just… so sexy. So sexy. I've never made anyone moan before. *Oh,* that *sound.* Oh, hell. It's coming, and it's going to be good.

But is she going to…? I need her to…

Oh God, please let her just…

Time for a Hail Mary maneuver. Maybe if I reach down and touch her there. Wait… how do guys do this? My arm is stuck. I can't get out of my own way. Wait. Okay. Right *there.*

Winning! Yeah!

Almost.

C'mon, Seabiscuit!

But… ahhhgghhmmm. Feels incredible for me, too.

Mayday! This train is pulling out of the station.

Can't. Hold. Out. Much. Longer.

CHAPTER 17
KATIE

The look on your face
Sweet and intense
Shreds my heart
Now I'm tilting fast
And spinning hard
All of me
Is lost to you

CHAPTER 18
ANDY

COMPLETE LOSS OF BRAIN FUNCTION
Please stand by…

CHAPTER 19
KATIE

FOR A FEW MINUTES we just lay there, breathing hard, while dance music continued to vibrate the bedroom wall. Andy's face was stuffed half into the pillow, half into my hair. I could feel the rapid rise and fall of his chest against mine.

But eventually the music stopped, and the silence seemed to bring the two of us back into focus. It was quiet enough to talk now, only I didn't know what I wanted to say.

Even for someone like me, who really liked sex, the part afterward was a little awkward. There was always that uncomfortable moment when your brain came back online and reminded you that you should probably untangle yourself from this sweaty boy and go on with your life.

The realization that special moments didn't last was always a disappointment. And the more special they were, the bigger the letdown.

This one was kind of a doozy.

Andy had gotten his breathing back under control, and was now playing with a lock of my hair. "Can I ask you something?" His voice was muffled.

"Yeah." Or *yes*. (Sorry, Mother. Though, come to think of it, after what I'd just done — stripping this boy naked and practically leaping on him — the use of "yes" versus "yeah" was a moot point. Right, Mom?)

"What I need to know is…" he hesitated. "Do you feel a sudden compulsion to begin dating women?"

What?

"*Oh!*" I began to laugh.

"Be honest," he said, turning his head to show me his smiling eyes. "Do you have an urgent desire to run out for a copy of the *Sports Illustrated* swimsuit edition?"

Laughing, I realized that this boy was just going to keep on surprising me. "Well, now that you mention it… I do find myself wondering whether I should date someone who shares my taste in lipstick."

First, he gave my ass a pinch. Then he pulled me close, and I snuggled into his neck. For a few minutes, his hands gently skimmed my back. But eventually, he smoothed my hair down and sighed. "I really don't want to move. But I have to get up and get rid of this, um…"

Condom. Right. I released him, though I didn't want to.

Rolling off the bed, he grabbed a tissue from the box on his desk, then stood in front of the wastepaper basket, his back to me. I used the moment to marvel at how long his legs were. And the fact that he had a really nice butt for someone so slim. Go figure.

"I should really go," I said.

When Andy turned around, he was frowning. "Oh, no you don't," he said, giving his head a little shake. "Not so fast." He came back toward me, and I tried not to stare at his nakedness. There was something really sexy about that long, lean body. He was built as if only the best, most essential parts had been added to his frame. As if any extra would just be a distraction.

On his way over, he snagged his boxers off the floor and stepped into them.

I'd pulled the sheet up to cover myself, and now he gave me a little nudge to move over for him. Dorm beds were pretty narrow. But I scooted toward the wall, and he slid into the bed, rolling onto his side to face me. "Hi," he said.

"Hi." I clutched the sheet against my chest. I was feeling very naked all of a sudden.

"I thought if I trapped you in here, you wouldn't go."

"You'll want me to, eventually," I pointed out. "If I'm still here a week from now, that would just be weird."

"Well," he cleared his throat. "If you say so. But we could probably compromise on tomorrow morning, no?" Beneath the sheets, his toes wandered over to be with mine. He trapped the arch of my foot between both of his and gave it a squeeze.

I didn't know what to say. My football player boyfriends had always complained that they couldn't *possibly* spend eight hours crammed into a tiny bed with me. "You won't sleep well. And there are exams to study for."

He gave his head a shake. "That's not the point. I want the whole package. We're supposed to have that tricky night's sleep, where I'm trying not to give you a black eye when I roll over. And I believe I'm entitled to some awkward conversation in the morning."

"Seriously?" I fought off a grin.

"Seriously." He leaned over to kiss my eyebrow, and then had to turn away so he could yawn.

It was catching, so I yawned too. "The problem is that I only have a dress to wear. Walking home tomorrow morning…" I let the sentence trail off. Because he'd understand what I meant. Anyone who saw me would know I was doing the Walk of Shame.

It was called that for a reason.

Andy frowned. "I have sweats you could borrow."

I pointed across the room at my spike heels, lying on the floor where I'd shed them so hastily a little while ago.

He chewed on his lip for a second. "Okay. I'll walk you home right now, if that's what makes you the most comfortable," he said. "Otherwise, I can set my alarm for seven. But we'll probably wake up then anyway, after elbowing each other all night." He gave me a shy smile. "And we could walk you home before anyone else even thinks about waking up. Then I could wait at the coffee shop while you shower and change. And *then* we'll get the earliest possible start on memorizing two hundred European paintings."

"Hmm," I said, as my heart gave a little flutter. That all sounded too good to be true.

"There won't be a soul outside at seven in the morning. Especially during exams," he pointed out.

"You really want me to stay?" He was probably just being nice.

He gathered me up in his long arms. "I really, really do."

CHAPTER 20
ANDY

I FOUND a t-shirt for Katie to wear. Actually, I picked out my favorite one, which had an X-wing fighter on the front of it. And that made her laugh. And I *loved* her laugh, because it sounded a little bit out of control. Here was a girl who usually matched her hair band to her sweater. She looked pristine and put-together every time I saw her. But the sound of her giggle gave her away. It was riotous.

And *man*, my X-wing t-shirt had never looked so good as it did with her long legs sticking out from under the hem. I found her an extra toothbrush, too. And then I checked to see if the bathroom was empty, and it was. So Katie did the mini Walk of Shame into the bathroom to brush.

"Do you want the inside or the outside?" I asked when she returned, pointing at the bed.

"You first," she said.

I shut the lamp off and then climbed in, scooting all the way over to the wall. She got into bed then, gingerly. First, I pulled the covers up. Then I put my hands on her hips and pulled her closer to me. "Let me show you how this works best," I said, angling the pillow just so. I positioned Katie's back against me so that her head was level with my sternum. That way we both had some breathing room.

"Mmm," she lazed against me. "Okay. I think I get it."

Luckily it was dark, and she was facing the other way. So she couldn't see how big my dorky smile was just then. Seriously, you could probably see my teeth from space. Because I'd never been happier than I was right then. I had the girl of my dreams in my bed, curled up against me. I was optimistic that maybe this would become a thing. But that was probably getting ahead of myself, right?

I wasn't going to lie here and worry about it, though. No matter what happened tomorrow, I would always have this night.

"So," I prompted. "Which European paintings are we going to memorize first?"

"The medieval ones," she said immediately. "There aren't as many of those as in the Renaissance section."

"Good point," I whispered, smoothing my hand down her hair.

"I'm a little worried about the modern stuff," she confessed. "He covered it really fast. The Russians… I don't remember what any of those paintings look like."

"Like… *The Knife Grinder*? We can tackle those," I said. "You know that little sofa in the back of the coffee shop? I'll park my butt on that puppy while you're changing. We can sit there and flip through the paintings on my laptop."

There was a pause, and I hoped she wasn't about to tell me that she'd rather study alone. "We are going to rock that test," she said instead. "We are going to kick its ass."

Again, I grinned in the dark. "We are going to send it home, crying for its mama." Katie giggled again, and I felt it in my chest.

Then it got quiet for a little while, and I wondered if she'd fallen asleep. I wasn't sure I even wanted to fall asleep. Because I didn't want to miss a moment of being with her.

"Andy?" she asked suddenly.

"Yeah?"

"Have you ever had a one-night stand before?"

Now there was a tricky question. "Well… I'm not sure I can say."

She turned to peek at me over her shoulder. "Never mind. That was a really personal question."

I dropped my arm around her waist and gave her a squeeze. "That's not the problem. It's just that I'm not sure. The answer is no. Unless I'm having one right now, and I was really hoping that wasn't the case."

After I said it, my heart nearly failed. Was that too much, too soon?

"You're definitely safe," Katie whispered.

Whew. I dropped my nose into her hair and took a deep breath of her. "Good to know," I said.

Her slim fingers gently stroked my wrist for a few minutes. And then she began to breathe deeply. I lay there smiling in the dark for awhile longer, until I fell asleep too.

And I had very, very good dreams.

EPILOGUE

DASH MCGIBB HAD a way of flipping his pen up in the air and catching it again. He did this while sitting in one of the old wooden lecture hall seats, waiting for the exam to begin. He flipped the pen a dozen times. Flip. Catch. Flip. Catch. It helped take his mind off of two uncomfortable things.

The exam was one of them. He'd taken this course because it had sounded easy. Looking at paintings — how hard could that be? And football season had ended only two weeks ago. That had taken up most of his time.

This test? It might go badly.

Also, there was the matter of the empty seat next to his. Until a week ago, that seat was always occupied by the most attractive girl in the freshman class. But Katie Vickery had not appeared in class for the last two lectures. And Dash guessed that he was the reason why.

The other night at the party, she had seemed okay. She'd even spoken to him a little bit. (Something about party planning trucks with pigs on them?) He'd hardly been able to concentrate on their discussion, because he'd been freaking out.

Because she *knew*.

Somehow, she'd figured out the ridiculous prank they'd made him pull. He'd seen the knowledge of it on her face the moment she appeared beside the Christmas tree. Even though his frat brothers had told him that the girls never found out. They'd *promised* that it would be a secret, and that there wouldn't be a shred of evidence.

At least that last part held true. He sure didn't want pictures floating around campus of him getting…

Shit. It was such a stupid thing that he'd done. So colossally stupid.

And for what good reason?

She must have figured it out immediately. Because Katie wasn't the sort of girl who would skip the last two lectures. All he could do about it now was watch the door, hoping that Katie didn't blow off the final exam just because he'd been the world's biggest asshole. He didn't want that on his conscience.

There was plenty on it already.

The minutes ticked by, and he waited. At the front of the room, the teaching assistants set up a projector. They would show sixty paintings, pausing thirty seconds on each one. There had to be a few easy ones in there, right? He was hoping to see the Mona Lisa's odd smile, or maybe *The Last Supper*.

At last, Katie hurried through the door, her gaze sweeping the crowd. He lifted a hand to wave to her, to let her know that he'd welcome having her as his seatmate. Even though she probably hated him.

Her gaze slid right on past.

Dash watched as Katie scanned the room, a ripple of uncertainty on her face. Then that ripple broke into a shy little smile, which she directed at a lanky boy two rows up. Wait — he was the basketball player. Her date from the other night.

The guy sat up straighter as she approached. Katie had that effect on people. They wanted to be just a little bit more of whatever they were when she was around. Dash had felt the same way. It's just that he'd never figured out what to do about it. Katie scared the shit out of him most of the time. That's how he always ended up slipping into the lowbrow humor of his frat buddies. He knew it wasn't the right way to talk to her. It's just that he'd never figured out what to say instead.

Looked like he'd never get that chance, now.

She scooted into the row where the basketball player sat.

Following exam day rules, she didn't take the seat next to his, but left an empty one between them. Still looking a little awkward — maybe even sheepish — Katie lowered her bag onto the empty chair, then turned to face him.

The basketball player reached a long arm behind the empty chair to give her ponytail a playful tug. And Dash saw Katie's smile melt into something warmer and less self-conscious than it had been a few seconds before.

"I wanted to ask you to lunch," the guy said. "But my bossy sister is going to be waiting for me in her car after the exam. She's my ride to New Hampshire."

"We'll go for lunch after the break," Katie said. "Three weeks from now."

"Yeah," he agreed. "But that sounds like a long wait to me."

Her face got soft then. And Dash didn't recognize that expression. He wondered if she'd never shown it to him, or if maybe he hadn't recognized it when he'd had the chance.

"I almost forgot," her date said, reaching to the floor for what turned out to be a tiny little gift bag. "This is a good luck present. For the exam."

Her eyes sparkled as she took the gift in two hands. Reaching inside, she removed two long, thin objects. "They're… a lightsaber pen and pencil?"

"Those are really good luck."

Katie giggled. "Because the force is with me?"

"Now you're getting it. There's one more thing in that bag."

Katie reached inside one more time, removing a little green thing, which she balanced on her palm. "It's Yoda."

"He's wise. And he also erases," the basketball player said.

She laughed. "That's… they're perfect. Thank you."

"It's nothing," was his reply. But obviously that wasn't true. Because Katie arranged those funny things on the little wooden writing arm of the lecture hall seat, then smiled at them as if she'd been given a set of crown jewels.

Dash flipped his very ordinary pen up into the air again, puzzling over what he'd just seen. He knew that girls liked flowers, which he'd never really understood. Flowers were expensive and they looked really sad when they began to wilt. But a Star Wars pen? *What the everloving fuck?*

It was almost exam time, though. A graduate student had passed a stack of test booklets down the aisle. Dash took one and passed the rest of the stack onwards.

"Quick," Katie said. She handed the basketball player a bulging gift bag.

From inside, he pulled… that awful pink basketball he'd been playing with the other night. Then he put a hand over his mouth and laughed.

Katie beamed at him. "It made me think of you. Sorry. There's something else in the bottom of the bag."

He pulled out a large bar of gourmet chocolate. "Hey… salted caramel!"

"Because we didn't make it to the ice cream shop." After she said that, her ears began to turn pink.

"Right," he chuckled. "I was really broken up about that."

"I'll bet," she said, looking toward the proctor, who was passing out the actual test now.

"Thank you, Katie," the basketball player said. He put his gifts on the floor and smoothed the test down onto the tiny desk in front of him. "And good luck."

"May the force be with you," she replied.

Dash looked down at the test he'd just been handed. It was time to stop worrying about Katie, and start worrying about European art. The painting identifications were tough, but probably not a total disaster. The essay question he chose took a long time, though. And by the time he'd finished comparing the Baroque period to Renaissance painting, he was one of the last people left in the room.

Tired now, Dash gathered up his things and turned in his exam booklet. He shook out his cramped writing hand and headed for the door.

He had managed not to think about Katie for ninety minutes. But that streak ended when he exited the building.

The basketball player was just tossing a duffel bag into the back of a car. Then he chucked the pink basketball inside too. Turning to Katie, he opened his arms.

With a sweet smile, she stepped in close and hugged him.

Looking away, Dash punched the traffic button to activate the crosswalk. (And did those buttons really do anything, anyway? Or were they just a way of asking for your patience while cars kept rolling by?)

Out of the corner of his eye, Dash could still see Katie and the tall guy. They were kissing now. But "kissing" didn't even do it justice. They were kissing each other as if they'd just invented it. She'd risen up onto tiptoes to reach him. And his arms encircled hers as if he were holding a rare and precious thing.

The look of pure absorption on the guy's face did something to Dash's gut. He'd once held five feet and four inches worth of perfection in his arms, and he hadn't tried even half as hard to hold on to it.

Now that seemed like an error. A big one.

The car that the happy couple leaned against gave a loud and impatient blast of its horn. They broke off their lip-lock, laughing. "I'll call you," the guy said.

"I hope you will," was Katie's answer. "Now go, before you get in trouble."

"I'm already in trouble," he said, opening the passenger door. He winked, folded himself into the car and closed the door. Katie gave him one more wave.

Dash glared up at the traffic light, willing it to change. Finally, it did. But he hesitated for a second anyway as Katie closed the distance to the corner.

I'm sorry. The words formed themselves on the tip of his tongue as she approached. He could say that, right? That was the thing he really needed to do.

Pedestrians moved forward, stepping off the curb. Including Katie. So Dash followed her, readying himself to speak to her once they'd crossed the busy street.

"Katie?" he said.

But she didn't turn around. She hadn't heard him. And now the trill of a cell phone rang out. Katie pulled her phone from her pocket, answering even as she walked down College Street. "Hi there." He could hear a smile in her voice. "I didn't think you meant you'd call *right away*," she giggled. Without a backward glance, she kept right on moving, her long strides carrying her up the street. Away from Dash.

He watched her until she well and truly disappeared.

T H E
E N D

STUDLY PERIOD

THERE ARE 1016 PEOPLE IN THE FRESHMAN CLASS AT HARKNESS COLLEGE.

I can't be the only socially awkward nerd girl virgin among them. Right?

It's time I learn to talk to guys without blushing and stammering. So I take a confidence-building job at the student tutoring center. Twelve bucks an hour, plus human interaction. What could go wrong?

A fun-loving French Canadian hockey hunk, that's what.

When Pepe Gerault sits down at my tutoring table, my brain shuts off and my mouth goes right into hyperdrive. Even the sound of my name on his lips—Josephine—gives me a mini orgasm.

I want to hand him my V-card. But all I manage to hand him is… my thesaurus. And my dignity. All seems lost, until I hatch a plan to get him alone…

Studly Period happens during the same school year as The Shameless Hour *and* The Fifteenth Minute

CHAPTER 1
SEPTEMBER

IT'S a quiet moment in the Harkness College tutoring center.

Okay—let's face it. They're *all* quiet moments at the tutoring center. But that's how we shy girls roll. We like the hush of whispered voices as the tutors pitch in to help. We like the walnut paneling and the pharmacist's lamps on each table. Each one makes a pool of warm light on whichever homework assignment has brought another student in for help.

My subject is English and writing. I was the only freshman to apply for a tutoring job, which means I'm often helping upperclassmen. That was half the point of getting this job—forcing me to talk to people.

Sometimes it's not so hard. I've just finished proofreading a junior's philosophy take-home test. She wore a Harkness Tennis jacket and diamond earrings. In other words, she's one of the attractive, sporty people. I call them the BPs, which is short for Beautiful People. But the paper was well-written and barely needed a second pair of eyes. So I can't hold her beauty and confidence against her. Not too much.

Now I have a free moment to myself, so I pull out my phone and open up the YipStack app to see who's online. My own most recent contribution has 26 likes and six comments. Not bad.

YipStack is my secret passion. It's a completely anonymous app that works by geolocation. So most every comment and every thread is from another Harkness college student.

I'd never heard of YipStack until my roommate suggested I take a look. She meant well. She was trying to prove to me that my acute awkwardness isn't all that rare. Unlike a real social network, YipStack doesn't bolster your popularity. It's anonymous, so it's more of a raw, unvarnished look at Harkness College.

But now I'm hooked. Besides Nadia, YipStack is my other best friend. I don't even tell her how much time I spend on the app, because it's more than a healthy amount.

I scroll through now, looking for some action.

Some yips are purely informational. *It is avocado and bacon wrap day at the student center. This is not a drill.* Some Yips are confessional. *I cheated on my Spanish quiz and now I'm just waiting for the cops to show up.* Beneath these little truth bombs are found a smattering of comments. Some supportive, some clever. Some grumpy.

Reading YipStack, it's obvious that not everyone at Harkness is perfect or even perfectly happy. They're tired or they're worried or they're out of time. They're drunk or sad or horny.

It's quiet tonight on Yipstack, too. *All the washing machines in Turner house are out of order. Guess I'll have to give all my dollar bills to strippers instead.* And, *If you're into weak beer and handsy men, Beta Rho is having a party tomorrow.*

Lovely.

Ah, and here's a familiar chestnut that gets yipped at least once a week. Not clever, but always popular: *When's the last time you had sex?*

The comments below are comforting to me, because they range from some overachiever's answer: *A half hour ago* to the more comforting *Two months ago or maybe three*?

I scroll down further, hoping to find my favorite response. *Never.* Because that's my answer too. After sifting through a couple dozen other comments, I finally find someone else who's still a virgin, too.

Phew.

It's nice to know I'm not the only one. Some of us are just too shy to make it happen. In high school, my equally nerdy boyfriend was also shy. Neither of us ever got up the courage to go there. We're both still virgins.

Or maybe he isn't anymore. I'm not about to ask.

With a quick glance around the quiet room, I begin to draft my next clever Yip. Writing is easier for me than conversation. I can be clever and self effacing as long as I don't have to look anyone in the eye.

First draft: *When Joan d'Arc was my age, she was brave enough to lead troops into battle. So why am I so nervous about going to a pizza party in the Beaumont common room tonight?*

Hmm. The joke isn't sharp enough yet. I delete the second sentence, changing it to: *So why do I have to rehearse three times just to order a pizza?*

That's better. And also true. I want to eat free pizza tonight, but if anyone tries to talk to me, it won't go well…

"Bonjour." The deep voice—from right above me—startles me so badly that I jump. My phone goes clattering to the desktop as I whip my chin upward to see whomever snuck up on me.

"*Désolé!*" he says. "I should come back later?"

"No," I say, fumbling my phone back into my bag. "Please sit down."

My heart is banging against my ribs, and not only because he startled me. If possible, I'm even more awkward with men than with women. It's worse if they're attractive.

And this guy? *Very* attractive. Wow. He has a wide, handsome face and coal-dark eyes ringed by impressively thick lashes, and a broad face. Broad shoulders.

Broad *everything*. Wow. He must eat a lot of protein. And now I'm staring as he arranges himself in the chair opposite me and draws out a folder. He's really handsome. One of the BPs, for sure.

I can't stop staring. There's something rugged about him that's hard to describe. There's color in his cheeks—at least the part that's not covered with dark scruff. And his biceps bulge from the sleeves of his T-shirt. He reminds me of a superhero going incognito, concealing his identity among the ordinary college students.

Though the muscles can probably be explained by the logo on his T-shirt—*Harkness Hockey*.

It's always the jocks who need tutoring. I swear. Nadia and I have a disagreement about this. She says that jocks are just used to coaching, and thus accept help more readily than the general population.

"I think they're just not as smart," I always tell her.

She just shakes her head. "You say that, but you're still intimidated by them. So which is it?"

Indeed.

"How can I help you," I whisper up at this handsome giant.

He frowns, and then folds massive hands onto the desk between us. "Excusez-moi?"

People always tell me my voice is soft, and that I'm hard to hear. He must agree, because he leans forward, those big, dark eyes blinking in close proximity. It doesn't help the knee-knocking, teeth-rattling nerves that overtake me whenever a beautiful man looks at me.

Get a grip, Josie. "How can I help you today," I ask carefully.

"*Bon.* I have the paper due for English. And my English is not so excellent. So I hope you will help me find all the places I fuck it up. I bring it…" He opens a folder and rifles through some papers.

For a long moment I just blink at him. "Your English…" Did he just say that he didn't speak the language?

"When I come to Harkness last year? I don't speak much English at all," he says, dropping a rough draft of an essay on the table between us. "Please help me find *zhe* places where I fuck up the grammar."

His honesty has stunned me. The Harkness students I've met so far would never admit to any kind of weakness. In fact, they tell me that most students wait until their grades are in jeopardy to find the tutoring center at all.

And I don't blame them. Struggling? That's shameful. Harkness is a top-notch school where everyone worships at the alter of intellectual exceptionalism. With an admissions rate that hovers around nine percent, having a big brain is the only way to get in.

Or at least I thought it was. Every year, something like a thousand valedictorians get rejections from Harkness. Who would *dream* of implying that he isn't as qualified as the next student?

This guy.

I'm actually irritated now, because it burns me up to know that some of us sweated every quiz and assignment in high school, because we needed our grade point averages to be perfect hundreds. But students are admitted to Harkness because they're really good at shooting a rubber disc into a net with a stick?

Apparently the English language is optional for athletes.

I pick up my red pen and begin with the first paragraph of his essay. All sophomores are required to take a writing seminar. And now I know why. Every sentence of his essay has an error. The essay is about his birthplace in Quebec. The ideas are well organized but the grammar is just awful.

"Hey, miss…" he pauses. "I do not catch your name."

"It's Josephine." And now I feel like a jerk because I never gave it to him.

"*Jhosephine*," he says, softening the J. My name sounds beautiful in his French accent. "I am Pepe. *Enchanté*. But why do you make *home town* two words here but not here?" He points at the changes I've made.

"Ah. In the first case, *home* is modifying *town*. But in the second case you're using *hometown* as an adjective. *Hometown memories*. So it's one word."

He frowns, and looks exceptionally handsome doing it. "That is confusing. Homework is always one word, even when it's a noun."

"True."

"Why?"

"Um…" I click the button on my red pen a few times. "Convention."

He looks skeptical.

I push on, because watching his handsome face is making me nervous. I edit the heck out of his essay, fixing the awkward bits and the errors. It's probably too much for a first-pass. I should make suggestions and let him work on it.

But he makes me twitchy, with his cheerful smile and tight T-shirt. He leans in to watch me work, and I'm actually sweating.

"How is this?" he asks, putting a broad finger on the page next to an edit.

His hands are enormous. I don't even know why I notice that. I have no business thinking about his hands. Or what his touch might feel like…

What is *wrong* with me?

He's waiting. Watching me. And I realize I didn't answer his question. Swallowing hard, I look down at the page.

Right.

"So…" I clear my throat. "You can't write about a blue small doddering fishing shack. It has to be a doddering small blue fishing shack."

"Why?"

"Um…" A bead of sweat rolls down between my breasts. Because I don't actually know why my order of adjectives sounds better. "Let me think for a second."

"They *all* modify shack," he points out.

"True…" Lord, it's hot in here. "But, uh…" My mind is a blank. I have been speaking English my entire life. And I have no idea why adjectives sound correct in one order and nutty in another. "Let's try another example!" I can do this, right? "Okay—the *tight blue hockey T-shirt*."

"You think my T-shirt is tight?"

My gaze flies up to find him grinning at me. "No! Just… We use, uh, size before color."

He grins. "*Size* before color. Got it."

Kill me! Kill me! Kill me! "Right Here's one—it's not *green small spiny dragon*." I'm babbling terribly. "It's a *small, spiny green dragon*."

He laughs, revealing dimples, and I lose another 10 IQ points. "Show me this dragon. I want to see for myself."

Oh, man. The moment he sat down at this table my brain turned to glue. The only way to recover is to get rid of him.

Lowering my head, I finish my edit at top speed. By the time I pass Pepe's essay back across the table, it's covered in red marks—like a bad case of road rash.

Maybe I'm not cut out to be a tutor. I should apply to be a professor's assistant instead. Whenever I make eye contact with Pepe, I'm uncomfortable. He's so handsome that it's like looking directly into the sun.

And now I've *savaged* his paper, even though I couldn't give him good answers to the only two questions he asked. Some tutor I'm turning out to be.

"Can I have an email address or a way to text you?" I croak. "I need to send you the rule for adjective order, so you know how to apply them. Sorry I couldn't explain it better."

He looks surprised by this apology. *"Pas de problème, Jhosephine."* He startles me by picking up my red pen, and then *my hand*. My mouth falls open as he writes his phone number on my palm.

His hand dwarfs mine, and I can't look away. Or speak.

"Bon." He stands up, and I'm so flustered I actually stand up, too. "When *zhe* new term starts, it always takes a while to get my English back. You have been much help!"

A lot of help, my brain corrects. Luckily, I don't say it aloud.

And then he shocks me again by leaning over the table to grab me into a quick hug. My entire body is briefly enveloped in bulky warmth. I inhale the scent of warm boy and clean hockey shirt. The scruff on his cheek scrapes my forehead, and goosebumps rise up all over my body.

Then, just as quickly, it's gone. He steps back and gives me a cheerful wave. "See you next week!"

I just stand there on my side of the desk feeling shell-shocked while he makes his exit. It's a long minute or two before I finally remember to sit down again.

That night, when I check YipStack before shutting out the light, I see this:

TIL there is no such thing as a green small spiny dragon.

I fall asleep smiling, and dreaming of men with large hands and dark eyes...

CHAPTER 2
SEPTEMBER / OCTOBER

TEXT TO PEPE GERAULT:

HELLO, this is Josephine, the English tutor from yesterday. I have a couple of notes for you.

1. After you left, I investigated the usage of "hometown" vs. "home town," and discovered that either usage is acceptable in adjective form. My sincerest apologies for any confusion that I have caused.

2. The rule for adjective order in a sentence is: a) opinion b) size c) age d) shape e) color f) origin g) material h) purpose.

3. Thank you for your patience with me yesterday. I wasn't in top form and I failed to answer your questions correctly. If you need further assistance there is a senior—Robert Kravitz —who works the evening shift on Thursdays. I'm told that he has swallowed the Chicago Manual of Style and can always cite usage rules on the first try.

Best of luck! —Josephine

TEXT TO JOSEPHINE ALLISTER:

Chaton—Thank you for these rules. I thank my a) cute b) little c) young d) slender e) brunette f) American g) English tutor for putting up with my bad writing.

I don't know if Robert Kravitz should have swallowed that book because that sounds uncomfortable. And anyway I have a double practice on Thursdays. Which days of the week do you work? I should like to bring you my next essay as soon as I write it.

TEXT TO PEPE GERAULT:

I work Monday, Wednesday and Friday from two to seven-thirty. But the tutoring center is open seven days a week, and there is always an English tutor on duty.

TEXT TO JOSEPHINE ALLISTER:

Magnifique! I shall try to find you on Monday. Hockey practice makes everything difficult, so I may need to wait until Wednesday. Cheers, *chaton*!

EMAIL TO THE WORK-STUDY JOBS OFFICE

Re: Job placement
Dear Ms. Allen,

You had mentioned that English majors sometimes work for professors. I would like to add my name to the list of interested candidates.

I am currently working in the tutoring office, but finding all the new faces a little challenging for an introvert. Also, it's my dream to work with Professor Sarky. She is really inspiring and I would love to assist her.

Thank you for keeping me in mind,

Sincerely,
Josephine Allister

EMAIL TO JOSEPHINE ALLISTER

Re: Job placement
Dear Miss Allister,

I am happy to put you on the waiting list for a professor's assistant job. But those are in high demand. Meanwhile, perhaps the face to face interactions at the student center will help prepare you for other challenging work!

All my best,
Deborah Allen

These days, each tutoring shift is more difficult than the last.

Sometimes Pepe shows up with an essay for me to read, and sometimes he doesn't. Either way I become a fidgety, nervous wreck wondering if he'll appear.

Or is that nervous, fidgety wreck? I can't think when I'm watching the door of the tutoring center. It's like waiting for the jump scare in a horror movie.

Some days he doesn't show, and I go home relieved, but strangely disappointed.

Other times he sits down in front of me, handing over an essay with limitless errors. The next half hour is always a trial, as my poor, stuttering brain tries to clean up the literary equivalent of a major oil spill while my hormones shift into overdrive.

Twelve bucks an hour doesn't seem like enough anymore. I should get hazard pay for the way he limits my executive function with his muscular body and his throaty laugh.

It's bad. Really bad. Last week I almost wrote "biceps" in the margin of his essay instead of "bilingual."

Two weeks have passed since our first, disastrous encounter, and I'm biding my time with only twenty minutes left on my shift. There's been no sign of Pepe all afternoon.

But then the door swings open and I know even before I look up that it's just admitted a set of wide shoulders in a hockey jacket.

With forced casualness, I mark my place in *The Complete Works of Shakespeare* and close the book. Meanwhile, my heart leaps up and down like a frisky puppy.

Down, girl.

Pepe Gerault pulls out the chair in front of me and sits. Then a big smile spreads across his broad face. "Salut, Josephine."

My senses begin to hum just from the sound.

"Comment ça va?"

"Bien," I manage. "Et toi?" And now all my French is exhausted. So I just stare at him for a minute, like a ninny. My eyes land on the slant of his masculine jaw, where dark scruff seems to be a permanent fixture. The color deepens at the cleft in his chin. I'd spent much of last week wondering what it would feel like to run my hands over that rugged face.

I don't know why that turns me on. It just does.

Then he removes his Harkness Hockey jacket to reveal… The tightest T-shirt I have ever seen. He must have painted it on.

Now he's just fucking with me. I'm pretty sure.

But it's working. His handsome mouth is moving, and I can barely concentrate on the words that are coming out. "So, *Jhosephine*," he says in that sexy voice. "Can you help?"

"Of course," I slur.

He slides another essay across the table, and I pick up my red pen. Today's topic is Holiday Traditions. I get to work, finding all the little inconsistencies. "Hmm…" I say, crossing out a verb. "We've been over mass nouns. The word family takes the singular verb form, not the plural."

"*Désolé*," he says with a smile. "I get it next time."

He drives me crazy. I wish I was half as relaxed about my short-comings as he is. "Can I ask you a question?" I surprise us both by setting my red pen on the desk.

"Yes?"

"What did you do about term papers last year? You said this was the first term you came to the tutoring center."

"Ah," he says, giving me a cheerful nod. "Most classes, it doesn't matter."

"It doesn't?" The professors give him a free pass on bad grammar because he's an athlete?

Pepe leans over and pulls out a notebook. "Most of my homework is like this." He flips open the notebook and sets it in front of me.

And it's…gibberish. Well, it's written in a language I don't speak: math. I'm staring down at a proof of some sort. But there are very few actual words. It's all variables and the occasional greek symbol.

"Math," I say, suppressing a shudder.

He tells me the exact type, but all I catch is "multi-variable."

"I see."

Pepe shrugs. "I take all math and science last year, plus beginning Italian and French lit. First year in a new country. Seemed like English could wait. But now I'll have English every term until I die." He grins. "Please don't quit your job, *chaton*."

Chaton. The second syllable drops from his throat sounding low and purely French. It's his nickname for me, and it means "kitten." I've never asked why he calls me this, because I don't want to hear him say that he uses it for all his female friends.

My raging crush knows no bounds.

I go back to editing his essay, feeling sheepish. Pepe is a hockey jock *and* math genius. And—me being me—that knowledge makes both my shame at dismissing him and my lust burn brighter.

He sits back in his chair and folds those muscular arms across his rippling abs. I can see them in my peripheral vision whether I want to or not.

"It's not that bad," I say quickly. "And the professor didn't give you much to work with. Let's just review all the forms of the present tense in English. And I think gerunds are tripping you up."

"Thank you, chaton," he says ruefully. "It will be a long semester. I hate writing. Even in French."

"Really? I love it, because writing gives me the chance to say exactly what I mean. It's easier than talking, because I can edit out the stupid shit. It's so much less embarrassing."

I know I've said too much because his bushy eyebrows lift in surprise. "Talking is embarrassing?"

"It can be." *Like right now.*

He shrugs. "Talking I can handle. Writing makes me sweat."

I try not to think about Pepe sweating, because the image is entirely too appealing. "What comments did the professor make on the last one you turned in?"

Pepe chuckles. "He said I need to broaden my vocabulary. That I use the same words too often."

"Yeah? That's an easy fix. Here." I root around inside my book bag for a moment until I find my old, battered paperback Roget's Thesaurus. "Here," I thrust it at him. "Use this."

For a moment he just stares at the cover. "It's yours."

"Sure. But you can have custody for the semester." It's a strange offer. My father gave me that thesaurus in ninth grade, the year before he died. It's not something I should give away. But Pepe and I are becoming friends. At least I think we are. I can loan him a book in his hour of need.

And Pepe looks touched. He opens the front cover, where he'll spot my father's name printed in faded pencil. Joseph Allister, Iowa State U.

"Use that if you're feeling stuck," I add, "Look up a word. Find a fun way to say whatever you need to say. Even one good one can change the whole piece."

"Thank you, *chaton*," he says with a big smile. "You make essay writing better."

The praise shouldn't light me up as much as it does. Did I mention I'm somewhat pathetic?

Three weeks later, I'm sitting in the student center with Nadia. This is our idea of a big night out—studying in a public place. Tonight we got here a little too late to grab the prime real estate. We managed to snag two armchairs, yet no coffee table. So we've turned our chairs to face one another and propped our stocking feet up on each other's seat cushions.

It works.

Shakespeare's *Twelfth Night* is open on my lap, but I'm skimming YipStack. My latest post is: *The real "walk of shame" is cutting in the snack bar line at the Student Center.*

Funny 'cause it's true. I have 76 likes and 12 comments already.

As I skim all the other action, something catches my eye. *Men's Hockey Wins Exhibition Game At Northern Mass. Let's do it again for points, boys!*

I sit up a little straighter in my chair. It's just dawning on me that I could watch Pepe play hockey. I've never been interested in sportsball. But attending a hockey game sounds like a fun new way to drool over Pepe without him noticing.

Even though we've seen more of each other lately, I still turn into a babbling maniac whenever he sits down across from me in the tutoring center.

How does a girl find the hockey team schedule, anyway?

I'm poking at my phone, trying to answer this question when Nadia nudges my thigh with her toe. It's subtle. Like she's trying to tell me something.

I raise my eyes just as a group of guys wearing Harkness Hockey jackets approaches us, heading for the sandwich counter. Nadia knows something of my crush, but she's never met Pepe.

But there he is walking towards us, as if I've conjured him. He's laughing with his friends, though, and doesn't see me. My gaze locks on him like a laser, because I've never been cool.

"Nice," Nadia whispers. "Wow. He's the one with the super dark hair, right?"

"Shh," I hiss, nudging her leg with my foot.

But something about our exchange catches Pepe's eye. I watch with growing alarm as his gaze lands on me.

And then he smiles.

"Oh, my," Nadia whispers. "Now there is a hunk of man."

I can't even shush her because I'm frozen like Bambi in front of a speeding eighteen wheeler. Pepe slaps one of his friends on the back and points at me.

"There she *ees*!" he yells. "Smartest tutor at Harkness!" He sort of gallops in my direction. I don't even have time to brace myself before he leans over my chair, scoops me up into his giant arms and sort of whirls me around in a circle two times.

Holy god. It's a Pepe hurricane. I claw at his arm in fear, but he just laughs.

A moment later I've been set back onto my feet. But I'm blinking up at him, my glasses askew, and taking in the sight of three highly amused hockey players behind him.

Also, I'm flushed from head to toe from that incidental hug. Any bodily contact with this boy makes my heart race. If he actually kissed me I might just pass right out. "Hi," I manage to squeak.

"Dude," one of the hockey players says from behind Pepe. "This is your tutor?"

If possible, my blush deepens.

"She must be a saint to put up with your ass."

"Oui," Pepe says with a broad smile. "Very patient. *Jhosephine* is the reason I have a B in the writing seminar, not an F."

"Buy that girl a beer," says another player.

"At least," says another. "Pepe—are we gettin' in line, or what?"

"Goh," he says, waving them off. His accent is strong even on the one-syllable word. "I'll be right there."

His friends give me a wave and move toward the snack line, but Pepe is still standing here in front of me, blowing up my brain. "This is my friend Nadia," I remember to say, but only because she's standing beside me now, smiling like a lunatic.

"*Bonsoir*, Nadia!" he says. "I have a favor to ask, *chaton*."

"Whatever it is, I'm sure it will be nooooo problem!" Nadia chirps.

I'm going to have to kill her. It's a shame because she was a pretty good roommate. Never leaves her dirty laundry on the floor.

"Can I give you my essay right now? We are looking at tape tomorrow and I don't *theenk* I can get to you until right before your shift ends."

"Sure thing," I say, not looking at my roommate. The wattage of her smile is giving me a sunburn.

"So lucky I ran into you," Pepe says, digging into his backpack. He roots around, finally emerging with two sheets of paper. "Thank you for this. And maybe I can buy both of you ladies a beer this weekend. Our goalie is having a party after the game against Princeton." He grins. "You know where the hockey house is? Off campus?"

"We can find it," Nadia chirps.

"Awesome." He nudges my elbow. "Do I sound like an American if I say *awesome*?"

"Totes," I say in a more or less reasonable voice. But my brain is shorting out as I try to imagine myself at an off-campus hockey party.

"See you soon, *chaton!* I'll text you the address."

And then I'm watching his muscular glutes power away from us, wondering what just hit me.

"Sit," Nadia hisses, nudging me toward the chair.

I land on top of my Shakespeare book and have to stand up again to grab it from under my butt.

"A party!" she squeaks. "This is going to be epic. That's the night Pepe will help you out with your little *problem*."

"Nadia!" My stomach is suddenly full of buzzing bees. "Please don't refer to my virginity as a *problem*."

Her eyes widen. "But that's exactly how you referred to it yourself last night."

"Oh. Right." *Whoops.* But in my defense, I hadn't meant my virginity in and of itself. I'd meant my inability to speak in sentences to any man I was attracted to.

"I have a good feeling about this." She lets out a happy sigh. "He's so *nice*. Like a big man-puppy."

Before I met Pepe, I wouldn't have thought that could be a compliment. But I know what she means. He has a kind of happy enthusiasm that's sexy without ever being scary.

Unless you're me, and everything is scary.

"We are going to that party," Nadia says, picking up her Spanish book again. "And I'm going to do your makeup."

I can't even think about the party. Lots of people in a loud room? That's just not my event.

But, hell. I *want* it to be.

Could it be?

The whole idea makes me break out in goosebumps, and I can't tell if they're from fear or excitement. Probably both.

I pick up Pepe's new essay. I get out my red pen—a new one, because I used one up already, probably on Pepe's work.

This week's Sophomore Essay topic is "When I Get Home."

And when I read the first sentence, all the tingling, zinging hope inside me dies.

CHAPTER 3
NOVEMBER

I'M RACING across campus in the rain, almost late for my six-thirty dinner date. Okay, it's not a dinner date. I'll be on the clock for the Student Help Center.

But I really don't want to be late to meet Pepe.

Naturally, I failed to bring an umbrella when I left my dorm room this afternoon, and I'm regretting the oversight. I'm sporting a style we'll call the Wet Dog as I dash through the gates to Turner House. "Thank you," I call to the student who's let me in. Then I get another dousing of rain as I cross the courtyard toward the dining hall entrance.

Once inside, the race is over. But my hair is dripping on the old oak floorboards. I should try to find the ladies' room and blot the rain water from my hair…

"Oh, *noh!*" Pepe's deep voice exclaims behind me. I turn around, and he grabs my bag off my shoulder, giving it a little shake. "Take off your coat, *chaton*. You're soaked."

Face burning, I do as I'm told. He ducks into a shadowy alcove and I see him hang my dripping jacket on a hook.

"*Bon,*" he says when he returns. "Shall we?" He's still carrying my bag as well as his. They both look small on his big frame. Also notable —my bag is pink with black polka dots. It's totally girly. And Pepe carries it without objection.

He is the perfect man. And he belongs to someone else. I've been a little depressed since reading his "When I Get Home" essay. She was right there in the first line. *Marie*. His girlfriend goes to school near their hometown in Canada. Pepe misses her.

He was *quite* eloquent at describing how much. It was his best writing yet. I hated every word.

Coincidentally, I didn't force myself to go to that off-campus party he invited us to. Why risk humiliation to impress a guy who's already taken?

I follow him through the common room, towards the hubbub of dinner hour. We still have our tutoring sessions, at least. And the crazy thing is that I'm better at it now. Since I know I don't have a chance with Pepe, my tongue doesn't get so tied anymore. I can string sentences together reliably. It's much better.

But it's also worse.

The dining hall is busy, as always. But I love this room. Turner House is built in the Georgian style, with intricate white plasterwork and chandeliers hanging from the high ceilings. The tables are long, gleaming oak with tall, carved chairs pulled up to them. We join a short line of students waiting to enter the serving kitchen and I grab a tray off the stand, taking a moment to flick locks of wet hair off my shoulders.

"Thank you for meeting me here, *chaton*." Pepe smiles at me. And the way he cups my elbow for a quick squeeze makes me feel a little light-headed.

It still takes me a few minutes to settle down in his presence. I've still got it bad. "No big deal," I stammer. Last month he let it slip that he was sometimes forced to choose between tutoring and dinner. So now I often meet him at whichever dining hall is scheduled to be open late.

True to form, this room is full of hockey, soccer and football jackets, because the jocks all have lengthy practice sessions six nights a week. It sounds grueling as hell.

"How's your week been?" I ask as the line inches forward.

"Not the best." His face sort of shuts down then, in a very un-Pepe-like way. I'm trying to decide whether or not to ask why when the guy behind the counter says, "next."

Pepe steps aside to let me order first, and my cheeks heat for no reason at all except that I'm charmed by his old-fashioned manners. A quick glance at the offerings informs me that it's Chinese night. "I'll have, um, the chicken and broccoli, thanks. That's all."

After my plate is passed over the counter, Pepe gives the server a grin. "Hit me hard," is all he says.

"No problem, man." The guy in the paper hat begins piling food onto a plate. A layer of rice, followed by a mountain of chicken. Two egg rolls are wedged precariously onto the rim. "That's all I can fit," he says, passing the plate into Pepe's waiting hands.

"*Bien*. You are the best."

At the beverage counter Pepe fills four glasses with milk while I fill one with diet soda. I wait for him, because I don't know where he wants to sit. Another guy in a hockey jacket walks up and claps Pepe on the shoulder. "I heard the news, man. So sorry."

"*Noh*, it is fine," Pepe mutters. He picks up his tray and lifts his sculpted chin, indicating that I should follow.

We cross the dining hall to find an empty little table tucked into a corner. We always dig in first and tutor last, so I take a couple of bites and watch Pepe. There are circles under his eyes. "You look tired," I say before I think better of it. His smile is flat tonight. That never happens.

"Eh." He shrugs off the comment. "Listen, *Jhosephine*. I don't know about this new essay. I wrote it late last night, and now I want to tear it up."

"It can't be that bad," I say quietly. "You've been doing great." In truth he still makes a lot of the same mistakes in his writing. But he works so damn hard that I have nothing but empathy.

And then there's my crush on him, size XXL.

Now he reaches into his book bag and pulls out his folder. When he hands it over, though, he looks nervous. Then he grabs his fork and shoves another bite of chicken into his mouth.

Something makes me hesitate. "Pepe," I ask quietly. "Are you sure you want me to read this?"

He sighs. "I was very upset when I wrote it. I can't decide."

"Do you want to think about it?" Essays can be so personal. I know a lot about him from reading everything he writes for this course. Last month I read about the recent death of his Italian grandfather. Pepe had learned of his passing while riding the bus home from a hockey game in Boston. He'd cried all the way back to Harkness, apparently.

The theme of that essay was unexpected behaviors. Pepe hadn't expected his hockey teammates to understand his sadness. But apparently the entire bus had become misty eyed. Coach had asked the bus driver to pull off the highway at a Friendly's so he could buy them all ice cream to cheer them up again.

"Listen," I tell him. "Just because your professor encourages you to write personal things in these essays, it doesn't mean you have to do it."

"*Noh*. I don't care if the professor reads. It is not so great, though, to have my pretty tutor hear all the dumb shit in my life." He gives me a sad smile.

The compliment catches me off guard. Our gazes lock, and his expression is both vulnerable and still unreadable. "If it helps, there's plenty of dumb shit in my life, too."

He smiles, but it's a little sad. Then he points at the folder. "Just read. It is okay. I need the help. This one is very rough, I think."

"What was the prompt?" I ask, opening the cover.

His chuckle is dry. "Something that angers us."

I read.

Liars are the thing that angers me. Some lie for politics. Some lie while selling soap on the television. Those are impersonal lies, at least. But sometimes it is much worse. A woman can say she loves you and then take your best friend to bed while you are here at school, working for a better life, trying to keep all your promises.

My eyes fly to his, and he winces. "I should not write essays on the day I break up with Marie."

"I'm sorry," I say quickly. "Maybe you'll get back together, though."

Slowly, he gives his head a shake. "I am finished trying to make her happy. It cannot be done. Each time she feels like hooking up, she dumps me. That's the pattern. Only this time she skipped that step." He heaves a sigh. "For a year I try to make long distance work for us.

She breaks up four times, but then begs to have me back." He rolls his eyes, and I smile because it's so cute to see a big man do that. "Yesterday my buddy texts me a picture of her making out with my old roommate from Montreal…"

The noise I make isn't very glamorous, but it's heartfelt.

"*Oui*. So that is it for her. I cannot make her wait for me. She has to want to."

I have no idea what to say. Who would cheat on this sweet man? He's both attractive and genuinely nice. "That sucks," I whisper. "I'm sorry."

He shakes his head. "Sucks more that I wrote an essay about it. A bad one."

I turn back to his writing, my red pen in hand. I shove my tray aside and start marking it up. The grammar and spelling are worse than usual, as if he'd vomited these feelings onto the page without the usual care. It takes me a while to get through it, and my heart is splintering the whole time.

When I hand the paper back, he slaps it down on the table as if embarrassed. "Now finish your dinner," he says, and I notice his giant plate is already emptied. "I'll get the ice cream." He's off like a shot, eager to get off the topic of his heartbreak, I suppose.

When he returns, it's with two sundaes. He's sliced bananas over vanilla ice cream, and added nuts and chocolate sauce.

"Wow," I remark as he sets a spoon down beside me. "I'd better hit the gym tomorrow."

"No, *chaton*," he says. "This isn't food for feeling guilty," he says, waving his spoon at the ice cream.

"What is it, then?"

"Food for getting over the girl."

"I don't know, Pepe," I tease. "The ice cream binge is kind of a chick thing to do. Will it even work on you?"

He smiles at me over his spoon. "I will let you know. My essay is not the best, no?"

"You've written better sentences," I say, hoping he appreciates my honesty. "But your professor might care about passion as much as he cares about expression, I think. There are points for grammar, but also for bravery."

Pepe snorts. "Bravery?"

"Yeah. It takes courage to put yourself out there. This essay can be more raw than the others. I like this line…" I scan the page to find it. "Anger from betrayal is more combustible than any other kind."

"*Combustible*," Pepe says, licking his lips as if tasting the word. "I found it in your thesaurus, *chaton*. I looked up *burn*."

This makes me irrationally happy. "I *love* the word combustible. Well done, sir."

He smiles, and the twinkle in his eyes finally makes a brief appearance. And I put it there.

CHAPTER 4
DECEMBER

LIKE EVERYONE ELSE AT HARKNESS, I have just survived my last exam, and therefore my first semester of college. For once, I'm celebrating in an unusual way.

"My butt is frozen to this bench," my friend Nadia quizzes me during the third period of the hockey game. "Why are we here, exactly?"

"Because hockey is the great American pastime."

"That's baseball," she argues.

"Oh, is it?" I just smile.

"Don't get me wrong," she says, offering me a piece of her hot pretzel. "I approve of you getting out of the house. And I think Pepe is terrific. But you shouldn't gaze at him from afar. You should get up close and personal."

"I'm thinking about it," I admit.

I picked up these hockey tickets yesterday, after reading a post on YipStack that made my heart beat faster. *Everyone's favorite French Canadian hockey player is back on the market, ladies. He was last seen dancing on a coffee table at a hockey house party. It's every girl for herself.*

It's not like I think I really have a chance with him. He's so friendly to me, and I'll admit it confuses me at times. Pepe is like sunshine. He shines on everyone at once.

But a girl can dream. So that's what I'm doing now, in row G of the student section. We're playing Brown, and we're winning. Every time Pepe skates onto the ice, it's like there aren't any other players. I just watch him. He skates like he writes—more passion than grace. Each acceleration is explosive force.

Those powerful thighs. Wow. They're going to star in my dreams tonight.

Pepe is a defenseman, according to the program I picked up. I think that's why he skates backwards most of the time. His job seems to be getting in the other team's way. At top speed. Backwards.

There are only four minutes left on the clock, and the score is 4-1. I don't know much about hockey but I feel pretty good about our odds. When Pepe leaves the ice for another visit to the bench, I pull out my phone and compose a quick Yip.

Who turned up the heat in the hockey rink from icy to combustible? Is it weird to get turned on by a bunch of sweaty guys skating after a rubber disc and bumping into each other? Asking for a friend.

About two seconds later I get my first comment. *Oh honey me too. And they'll all be at Capri's Pizza after the game.*

"Nadia?" I ask my roommate.

"Yeah?"

"How do you feel about a trip to Capri's pizza?"

"Really?" she squeaks. "You know that's the hockey hangout bar, right?"

"I've heard," I say, with forced nonchalance.

A very loud buzzer sounds suddenly, signaling the end of the game. And since my hockey fandom is so new, the noise makes me jump about a foot in the air.

"Easy," Nadia says with a smile. "You really need to leave the dorms more often."

"You think?" I sniff, unlocking my phone again. Below us, the team is lining up to shake hands with their poor, downtrodden opponents. Then they file off one by one.

"Girl, get off YipStack," Nadia complains.

"I *am*. I'm texting Pepe." *Nice job tonight! So exciting to watch you win. TIL that eloquence takes many forms.*

Nadia and I are still putting on our coats when I get a reply. *You saw the game??? The win was already sweet, but now it's even sweeter, chaton.*

My heart does an awkward twerk inside my chest. "I feel like a slice would be really tasty right now."

"I'll bet you do." Nadia leaps to her feet. "Let's go! I'm sleeping at Josh's tonight. Just putting that out there."

"When has that ever mattered to me?" I ask, following the slow line of students up the steps toward the exits.

"You never know," Nadia insists. "Tonight could be the night."

Forty minutes later I pay for our beer at Capri's pizza and then look around for seats. The place is crammed with students blowing off steam as exams end and Christmas break kicks in. I lift our pitcher of unappetizing brew and hope to find a table that someone else overlooked. Someone jostles me, and I almost spill the beer.

"Sorry," a guy wearing his baseball cap backwards says.

This is why I don't go out. How is this fun?

A peek into the middle room reveals plenty of hockey jackets. But Pepe isn't there, damn it. Maybe he'll turn up soon? It's a struggle to hold on to the scrap of optimism which brought me here tonight. And all the tables in the hockey room are taken. Of course they are.

So much for the feminine ambush I was planning.

"Here," Nadia says, tapping my arm. "I see a place. It's quieter back here, too."

She leads the way into the back room, and the crowd thins. There are no hockey jackets back here, though.

Ah, well.

Nadia puts two plastic glasses down on our table and grabs the pitcher from me. She pours, then passes me one.

I take a sip and then make a face.

"That good, huh?" She takes a sip and rolls her eyes. "Okay, so we're actually here. And you're wearing mascara. You never wear mascara."

True story. "I'm really not sure why I bothered. Even if you-know-who spotted me back here, I don't know how to be that girl."

"What girl?"

"The kind who goes home with the guy. I wouldn't know what to say. And even if I did, I couldn't deliver it with the confidence required. I'm hopeless."

"You aren't," she says, the way a good friend does.

And maybe hopeless is too strong a word. But I'm bad at flirting, and I'm confused about whether I should. Lately, Pepe and I are closer than ever. Our dining hall habit has expanded to two or three nights a week. Sometimes I'll read his essay for five or ten minutes and we spend the rest of the time just chatting. And on the days we don't see each other, we often text. He'll send me a photo of a page in my thesaurus. *Shall I make the tacos in my essay tasty, delicious or delectable?* And I'll reply: *Any of those, but now I want tacos.*

Is that just friendly? Is it flirty? How does any girl know?

"We're friends," I tell Nadia. "But my foolish heart always wishes for more. And so here I am, hoping for a miracle. He just won a game, right? He's in a good mood. You have to make hay while the sun shines."

She touches her glass to mine. "You can take the girl out of Iowa, but you can't take the Iowa out of the girl." She glances over her shoulder. "Do you see him? I need clues so I'll know when to quietly disappear."

I lean all the way to the side and squint into the other room. Like that's not as brazen as wearing a sandwich board reading *Scoping Out The Hockey Team*. "Nope."

She takes another sip of her beer and then grimaces. "How did he get the name Pepe, anyway. Is he Italian?"

"His grandfather was. He's French Canadian."

Nadia grins. "You know his grandfather's name? Someone is a little obsessed."

"I've read his whole life story by now. Come on. I'm just a good tutor."

She smirks. "How long are we sticking with this man hunt? Do I get a slice of pizza out of it?"

"I'll buy us some," I say, standing. It will give me an excuse to case the other room again.

I head over to the pizza counter and ask for two slices. One of the Capri brothers slaps them onto thin paper plates, and I pay the five bucks I owe.

"*Chaton*," a low voice says into my ear, and I actually jump. When I turn, he is there. Pepe's hair is damp from the shower, and he wears a checked flannel shirt. A whorl of chest hair is visible just below his throat, and my eyes get stuck there, wondering what the rest of him looks like. "You come to Capri's?" he asks, looking gleeful. "Need a beer?"

"I have one…" I start to say.

"…Right here," Nadia finishes, appearing suddenly. "Here—trade you." She hands me my glass and takes her slice of pizza. Then she's gone before I can even thank her. Who knew Nadia was such a great wingman? I file that away to think about later.

Then I take a sip of beer, and my distaste must not be well hidden, because Pepe laughs. "That good, noh?" He waves at the Capri brother on duty. "*Bon.* Three slices and two glasses of your auntie's hooch."

Two small wine goblets appear on the bar, and a second later they are filled with a dark red wine from a brown jug. Pepe smacks a twenty onto the counter and smiles at me. "Drink up, *Jhosephin*." He hands me a wine glass. "To English grammar and homemade Italian wine."

"And to beating Brown. Cheers," I say, caught in his delectable smile. I take a sip, and the wine is spicy and a hundred percent more appealing than the beer. "I've never seen wine at Capri's before."

"Mario takes care of me." He cocks his head toward the pizza ovens. "His grandparents are Italian, too."

And now I'm more in awe than usual.

"Come, *chaton*." He gestures toward the room where the hockey players are gathered. "Unless you need to go back to your friend?"

"Well…" I look at our table in the back, and Nadia is already gone. "Lead on."

And just like that, I'm hanging out with Pepe at Capri's. Achievement unlocked.

Ninety minutes later I am tipsy, and having a blast.

Even if I never have Pepe the way I want him, this evening with him is everything. He's an attentive companion, introducing me to dozens of teammates. I wait for him to tire of babysitting me. Instead, he tucks me against his side and introduces me around.

"Trevi! *Jhosephine* is my super patient tutor!" And, "Rikker! Stop staring at your boyfriend a minute I have to introduce you to zhe smartest girl at Harkness."

And so on.

His arm around my shoulder makes my heart beat faster. So does the attention. The big Canadian has good looks and a mean slap shot, and *manners*. Every time he smiles at me I feel a little more warmth blooming in my chest.

The wine doesn't hurt, either. I drink a second glass, and then a third. Good thing they're small, because I have the tolerance of a flea. A nerd girl flea. If that's a thing.

But the best moments are when Pepe and I end up alone in a booth, our elbows on the table, talking about nothing and everything. He tells me about how quiet the campus was over Thanksgiving, when only the hockey team was here practicing, and I tell him about my mom's silly Christmas rituals, and about a second semester English seminar I'm excited for.

"No more essay class next term," he says. "I'm so relieved."

"Yeah?" I'm not relieved because next term he won't need me as much.

"*Oui*. I can't wait for New Year's."

"Fun plans?" I ask.

"*Noh*." He shakes his big head. "It will be a quiet night at home, seeing as I now have one less friend and no girlfriend. But I want the next year to hurry up. This past one wasn't so great." He touches his wine glass to mine. "To better times, *chaton*." His gaze is like a warm bath, his smile bright. Maybe every girl gets the same treatment, but I spend a happy hour or two pretending that it's all just for me.

Eventually the party begins to wind down. I don't know if it's the hockey victory or the fact that exams are over, but it looks like a big night for hookups. I watch couple after couple maneuver out of the room together, lip-locked and grappling each other like a pair of police academy recruits practicing their frisking techniques.

I'm fascinated and also jealous. I want to be the kind of girl who can just give Pepe a knowing smile and invite him back to my room. But while I excel at English grammar, I know very little about seduction.

And it's getting late. "I'd better get home," I say as yet another couple stumbles out together. "And you have a plane to catch in the morning, right?"

"Oui." Pepe props his chin in his hand and studies me. "Do you wish me to walk you home?"

The question catches me completely off guard. "Well it's not that far," I babble. And that's not an answer at all. I want to say *Yes! Walk me home!* But I can't make my mouth say the words, because then he will walk me home and I won't know what to say when we get to my door. I'll probably go with, *Have a great holiday!* Because I won't know how to close the deal.

I will *never* know how to close the deal. I'm going to die a virgin.

"Just tell me this." Pepe pulls his phone out of his pocket. He unlocks the phone and then opens...

Yipstack!

"This is you?" I watch with growing horror as he turns the phone around to show me the yip I wrote during the hockey game. The one where I admit to being turned on by hockey players. The one where the first comment tells me that Capri's is the place to go after the game.

"Yipstack is an-anonymous," I stammer.

"The word *combustible* is not," he says.

CHAPTER 5
DECEMBER

I WONDER how many synonyms my thesaurus knows for *embarrassed*?

I'll bet there are plenty. I can think of several off the top of my head. But *abashed, chagrined* and *sheepish* aren't really strong enough for the way I feel right now, as Pepe waits for me to confirm or deny my lust-filled post on Yipstack.

Mortified. Yeah, that sounds about right.

"Maybe the author does not want to say," he whispers. "But a pretty girl told me once that writing was easier for her than speaking. I hope if she has anything to tell me at least I would get a text to me directly."

"But that sounds excruciating," I blurt out, finding yet another word for this moment. "Texts can be ignored. Or laughed at."

He sits back a couple of inches. As if offended. "I'm not the kind to laugh, *chaton*. Don't you know that already? Just like you don't laugh at all those things I do wrong in English. That is not how it is with us."

Oh. I really like the use of "us" in that sentence.

"You're right. I'm sorry." I believe I've actually offended him. And I don't know how to untangle myself from this tricky place. I'm stuck in awkwardville, but I finally understand something important. Those girls who take the guy home with them? They don't have any special magic, or a secret playbook. It's just that they're willing to crash and burn.

And I don't think I am. Not with Pepe, anyway. That would hurt too much.

"I should go," I say suddenly.

"Ah." Pepe sighs. "Yes, okay." He stands up, too.

I retrieve my jacket from its hook in the other room. And then Pepe takes it out of my hands and holds it up so that I can more easily slip it on.

He is so polite that I can hardly stand it.

Then Pepe takes my hand in his. The slide of his thumb against my palm is the most distracting thing I've ever felt in my life. Is it weird that he's holding my hand? Do friends do that?

Sure they do, the wine in my bloodstream assures me. We walk silently out of Capri's, and down Wall Street until it joins College Street.

We turn left and walk another block. This is it. The bitter end of the semester. And I don't even know if Pepe is taking any English classes next term. If it's all math, I might never see him.

Reluctantly, I take my hand back when I'm standing outside the gate to Fresh Court. "Have a great holiday," I say in a shaky voice.

"You too, *chaton*." He smiles at me. "I will let you go. It is late."

"Right," I say slowly, my heart beating wildly inside my chest. It's now or never. If I crash and burn, I'll have three weeks to recover. So I walk to the edge of this cliff and I step off it. "Is it *too* late, though? For me? And you?"

His thick eyebrows lift in surprise. "Never."

Okay. Wow. "Walk me home?" My voice breaks on the last word, but I got the sentence out. Barely.

"Of course," Pepe says immediately. He takes my hand again and leads me through the gate. Fresh Court is ringed by historic dormitory buildings and old-fashioned gas lighting.

I choose the slate path which stretches toward my building. We don't speak. I don't know what will happen now, and I may still goof everything up. But for once in my life I feel brave. Taking a risk hasn't killed me yet, anyway.

The walk to my building takes just two or three minutes. Pepe's bear paw is wrapped around my hand, and I don't want to ever let go.

"Ah, you leef in Parker," he says as we reach my entryway door. "I stayed here last summer for training camp."

"The heat doesn't work all that well, does it?" I babble. "Wait. If it was summer then you didn't care about the heat…"

Big brown eyes measure me. "You are cold? I know *une solution*."

I don't even see it coming. He leans in to kiss me, and there's no time to panic. Those full lips brush mine, and they're even softer than I'd imagined. The woodsy scent of Pepe envelops me, and his scruff tickles the corner of my mouth. My entire body breaks out in goosebumps while Pepe makes a low sound of approval.

Then he slants his broad face, and the next kiss happens in slow motion. First there's a delicious pressure as our mouths find just the right angle. His kiss is firm and deliberate. The snick of his kiss makes me tingle. Everywhere.

I clamp my hands down on his shoulders because I don't want him to stop and I'm too stunned to say so.

And he doesn't. He kisses me again and again, right there on the doorstep. His lips part mine, asking permission. I open on a gasp, and his tongue sweeps inside. He tastes of red wine and tenderness.

Thunk goes my head against the door, and I have to grab his biceps to steady myself.

"*Attention*," he chides, cupping the back of my head. "Let's take you inside."

Hell yes. Let's. Except I'm suddenly sober as a judge and starting to panic. I still don't know my lines. My room key shakes in my hand as I try to think what to say. Do I offer to take his coat? Do I make more conversation? And then how to get more of those kisses?

Pushing through the entryway, I open the second door, and I've never been happier that Nadia has a boyfriend. Our room is empty. My hand finds the light switch on the wall and… I don't flip it.

My fingers hesitate on the switch plate as my eyes find Pepe's. And he *knows*. As my hand drops away from that light switch without turning it on, he steps closer. His hips bump against mine, and excitement pings through my insides.

I expect to get another kiss, but first he cups my chin and stares at me in the dim light.

The pause makes me nervous, and I hear myself blurt out a question. "Why do you call me *chaton*?"

"Aw, *chérie*," he says, his smile growing. "Because you are just like a...baby cat."

"A kitten?"

"*Oui*. Big eyes and timid." His hands land on my hips, and then his mouth dips right to my neck. I'm still trying to picture a kitten, but he's already begun making love to the sensitive skin just over my collarbone.

I shiver. "I'm not timid."

"*Noh*?" His tongue dips into the V-neck of my sweater.

"Definitely not," I babble, as electricity pings throughout my entire body. "Dunno why you'd say that."

"Good to know," he mutters, raising his chin, claiming my mouth with his bigger one. The next kiss is bottomless. In that moment I realize that I'd never been with a guy who knew exactly what he was doing. Pepe kisses me with great intention. I relax into the rhythm, overwhelmed by the cascading sensations I'm experiencing. Joy. Nervous anticipation.

Heat. So much heat.

"You have the most beautiful throat," he rumbles against my lips. His big hand comes up and a thumb traces a line from my chin to my breasts. "When you are telling me about the grammar rules, I just want to taste you right here."

Yes! Yes! Do it! With shaking hands I push his hockey jacket off his shoulders and it falls to my floor with a jingle. I need him to know that I mean business. So I reach for the buttons of his shirt. I spent the whole evening trying not to undress him with my eyes. He stops to watch me. I make quick work of all the buttons, and reward myself by placing a palm over the center of his fuzzy chest.

"Take it back," I say, my hand stroking his pecs. My voice sounds a thousand times more courageous than I feel. My naughty hand slides down over his abs, because I can't help myself.

"Take what back?" Hard muscles undulate beneath my hand, tempting me.

"I'm not timid," I insist again, probably more for my own benefit than his. I can do this, right? I can get very very naked with him and let it all unfold, like a brave girl who takes what she wants.

In answer, he grasps my wrist so my hand is now under his control. He sweeps my palm over the ridges of his abs, past the waistband of his jeans, until my palm covers his prominent erection. The noise I make is both shock and excitement. My other hand reaches out to grasp the side of his neck. I tip forward and place a kiss there, and then I kiss my way down to the hollow at his throat. And who knew I had a thing for chest hair? But it's *his*. It's an intimate glimpse of him I've never had before.

Touching him makes me so hungry.

With gentle hands, Pepe lifts my top over my head. As the cool air hits my skin, he kisses the juncture of my neck and shoulder. And it's as if all the nerve endings in my body realigned themselves to that spot.

I might become the first girl who's ever had a shouldergasm. Or maybe that's a thing?

Then his skillful hand slips down my shivery belly. He unzips my pants to dispatch them on the floor. I kick them off, trying for gracefulness and failing. Pepe steers me over to my bed and pulls me down with him. "*Qu'est-ce que tu veux, chaton?*" What do you want?

Just you. Like this. I pull him into another perfect kiss, because words have failed me. But I manage to open the button on his jeans, and unzip them. And Pepe makes the sexiest noise I have ever heard in my life. It's part moan and part curse, with a chaser of gratitude.

I guess talking isn't the only way to get my point across.

"*Chaton,*" he groans, swatting his clothing away. "*Tu es très belle.*"

Wowzers. Compliments sound twice as good in French.

Soon we're skin on skin, and I'm drunk again—on kisses, not alcohol. My body is crying out for more, but Pepe seems happy to kiss me all night long. I'm not complaining, either.

"*Jhosephine,*" he whispers against my lips. "I do not have a condom. I was not expecting to love you tonight."

That's an interesting way to put it because I think I love him *all* the time. Nevertheless, this is a problem I can fix. I wiggle away from him for a second, just far enough to reach over and fish the condoms out of my nightstand. Then I hand them to him.

I expect Pepe to be as quick with the condom as he was with all of our clothing. But that's not what happens. He's holding the strip of three in his hand, studying them. Then his brown eyes turn to me.

And I see hesitation there.

The strip in his hand is three condoms. Every first year student gets a set during orientation. They say Welcome to Harkness in a continuous stream of text across the strip. And, comically, there's a phallic print of the Harkness bell tower stretching across the trio. Some designer had a good time with that.

Mine have never been used. And Pepe—since he's clever about literally everything except for English grammar—has just made a leap of logic about why I still have these, and what it might mean.

"*Chaton*," he starts. "Are you sure that—"

I put a hand over his mouth. "Please," I whisper. And just in case that's not clear enough, I add, "It's your turn to be the tutor. That's all."

"Okay," he says. "*Bien*."

Everything is *bien*. I'm nervous but also happy as I lie back on the bed. I watch with wide eyes as Pepe suits up, his big hand rolling the condom down his…

Whew. It's hot in here. Maybe the heat works after all.

Pepe lies down, spreading his big body out over mine. "You make me so happy tonight," he rumbles into my ear. Then he is everywhere at once, with shameless hands and a wicked tongue. Kissing me. Stroking me. I wrap my arms around him and listen for every sweet nothing which falls from his mouth.

"Breathe, *chaton*," he says when the big moment arrives. I inhale, and he makes the most delicious noise as he joins us. It's only awkward for a moment, until he kisses me again. "*C'est bon, C'est bon*," he chants as we make love. "*Magnifique!*"

My thoughts exactly.

CHAPTER 6
JANUARY

THREE WEEKS later I fly back to Harkness for my second semester of college. But I'm not tutoring, and I'm not nearly as buoyant as I was at the start of the next term.

I really don't want to dwell on why.

With stacks of freshly printed syllabi under both arms, I trot up a set of marble steps of the English department building. The corridors smell of coffee and old books, and the scent is a balm for my soul. If there were more time, I'd stop right in the middle of the staircase and just inhale it, like the nerd that I really am.

When I reach seminar room 207, I open the door with my hip. Professor Sarky beams at me from under her spiky crop of salt and pepper hair. She is seated at the head of a gleaming walnut conference table, where fifteen or so college women have already gathered, each with a notebook open to a fresh sheet of paper. The air is tinged with first-day-of-the semester expectation.

This is just what I need after moping around my parents house for three weeks.

"Everyone—this is Josie Allister, my assistant," the professor says as I carry the stack of syllabi over to her.

I won't lie—my heart swells to hear her call me her assistant. This job doesn't offer me nearly as many hours as my tutoring gig. I'll miss the extra fifty bucks a week. But there are advantages to being Professor Sarky's assistant. In the first place, she's a legend in her field. She's smart and innovative and I look forward to helping her with whatever she needs, no matter how trivial.

Also? The tutoring office is dead to me now. I can't afford to come face to face with a certain hockey player again. Too embarrassing. Too heart-rending.

Moving on.

I sit down at the table and uncap my pen. It's a new semester, with a new slate of classes, and a new boss. *Let's do this.*

The professor opens the class with a heartfelt speech. "Thank you for joining me on this literary journey! The official course title for this seminar took me a while to craft. After many hours of contemplation, I settled on, 'The Romance Novel and its Modern Female Voices.'"

And now I love Professor Sarky even more for admitting that she's as indecisive as us ordinary mortals.

"I've been wanting to develop this seminar for a long time," the professor tells us. "I'm *sure* there are a few gentlemen in the English department who are still snickering." She beams at us to let us know she isn't bothered by that at all. "But romance is the single highest-selling genre of the literary world. That's meaningful to me." As she speaks, Professor Sarky passes my stack of syllabi around the table to her left.

"Since I began teaching here, Harkness has offered a popular course on The Bible as Literature. The catalog advertises it as a course about the world's *most-read book*. And that makes sense, right? But this semester we're going to study the language's most-read *genre*."

A polite chuckle hums throughout the all-female crowd. It's really no surprise that only women showed up for the course, which is cross-listed with the Women's Studies department.

"The romance novel has many critics," the professor points out next. "And—as in *any* genre—some of the books aren't as well-written as the classics. But that doesn't diminish the importance of their place in the bookstore. It is a genre written largely by women, for women. We're going to explore all the ways that romance novels are subversive. And we're going to discover what those books have to share about women's evolving voices over the past several decades."

I find myself leaning forward in my seat. This is why I came to Harkness—for this class, and this crazy, brave professor. Not to meet ungrateful men, but to study language and literature with lively minds.

And since real-life romance is a disappointment, at least I can read about it in books.

I'm in the midst of these encouraging thoughts as I notice the old brass doorknob turning. There's an unfortunate squeak, and Professor Sarky breaks off her introductory comments as we all watch to see which apologetic woman will enter and hastily take a seat.

Although. The shadow cast on the antique textured glass window is too vast to be a woman's. And when the door swings open I'm so startled I drop my pen. The figure who enters is the very man I'm avoiding.

"*Excusez-moi,*" Pepe says.

My eyes dive for the table as my cheeks begin to flame. The low, guttural sound of his French is like a melody I'd spent the last three weeks trying to forget. I only hope he'll leave the room before he spots me.

Because there is no earthly *way* a hockey player has decided to take an English course on romance novels. The locker room teasing alone would be a deterrent, right?

But when I raise my eyes again, he's still there, and taking a seat, too. In the silence he's caused by his tardiness, the only sound is the squeak of a chair on the old wooden floors as he seats himself.

"Good morning, sir," the professor says without letting her smile slip. "You have joined us during the introduction for English 217, The Romance Novel and Modern Womens' Voices. If this course was not in your travel plans, you may wish to take this opportunity to find the right room."

"*Oui!*" he says quickly. And even without looking at him, I can hear the cheery smile in his words. "Sorry for my lateness. This *eez* my first time at zhe English Department. I do not always find English words with the first try, and now the same *eez* true of the building." He beams at the professor, and I feel every girl in the room sigh a little.

Pepe's charm is infectious, damn him. I'm living proof.

And now my little bubble is burst. Two minutes ago, this room was a place where I hadn't made any mistakes yet. And now my biggest one is seated four chairs away. Professor Sarky begins to speak again, but my concentration is blown. I stare down at the syllabus with unseeing eyes, trying not to look at him. But his shoulders are so broad that they're inescapable in my peripheral vision.

I've just spent three weeks at home in Iowa trying not to feel bad that Pepe hasn't spoken to me since our big night together. I'm still trying to make sense of it. To me, that night was everything. To him, it was just a one night stand. A little stress relief after a difficult semester.

While the professor drones on about early twentieth century popular fiction, I sneak a quick glance at him, just in case I've overblown the attraction in my mind.

But this backfires, because his big, dark eyes are fixed on the professor with polite attentiveness. His sculpted jaw rests in one big hand, and once again I'm studying the shadow of his whiskers over that perfect face. I'd spent all of last semester wondering what it would feel like to run my hands over it.

Now I know what it feels like, and I'm more of a wreck than ever.

While moping my way through Christmas break, it occurred to me that not every girl would feel the same. Some women who'd enjoyed a perfect night in Pepe's company might feel unscathed.

My roommate agrees. "You said it was the hottest night of your life," Nadia reminded me, mid-mope. "Maybe a repeat wouldn't live up to the first time. Put that night on a mental pedestal and leave it there, untarnished."

It's a nice idea, with one big flaw. I *like* Pepe. All of him. The smiles and the manners and the grammatical challenges. I want to spend more time with him.

He doesn't share that feeling, though. After our post-exams sexfest, he left in the middle of the night, explaining that his flight left early the next morning and he hadn't packed.

I didn't panic, though. Perfect excuse to mash and dash, right? I fell into a blissful slumber and dreamt of our perfect future together.

The fairy tale ended the next morning at 9:30 when I opened my dorm room door to find my thesaurus on the welcome mat. When I saw it cast aside there, I just knew. I could practically hear his single-guy gears turning. *Well, this is gonna be awkward. Better ditch the book now so we don't have to speak again.*

Even then I wasn't quite ready to believe that Pepe would shut me out. I let a day go by, and then another. He didn't text me or call. But I'm a modern girl (if still a chicken) so I pulled up my big girl panties and texted him. After about sixteen drafts I went with: *Hi Pepe. Hope you're having a great vacation. Thinking about you! J.*

Now I regret it. Because I never got an answer back. Not one word.

Who does that?

"Jo? Josie?"

The professor's voice brings me suddenly back into the present. "Sorry," I stammer, horrified to find every set of eyes was on me. Including Pepe's. His brown eyes regard me so seriously that I have to wonder if he can read minds.

Professor Sarky grins. "You can go ahead and explain the library now."

"Right," I say, and it comes out sounding froggy. I clear my throat. "The, uh, cart has fifty romance novels on it. They're sorted according to decade. This is just the first shipment. I'm expecting books from a dozen used booksellers, as well as orders from Amazon and Walmart."

"This will be the first time that Harkness has ordered teaching texts from Walmart!" The professor announces with glee. "I am making history."

I paste a smile onto my face and finish my speech. "Each week, you should plan to take two or three books home. Prof. Sarky has prepared an online survey form where we're going to catalog our impressions of the romance genre over time. The survey form will help you record details such as character names and occupations, tropes and archetypes. Details like that. You'll find the URL on the syllabus."

Until a half hour ago, I was thrilled to be part of this little research project. Now I can't wait to get out of the room.

Pepe's hand shoots into the air.

"Yes sir," the professor says.

"Are we to read the whole book? Or just inspect?"

"It depends." Professor Sarky taps the syllabus. "As outlined in here, you will read at least five romance novels over the course of our time together. Three will be classics that we'll read together, like Samuel Richardson's *Pamela*. Two will choose yourself, and the rest you will merely catalog." The professor lifts a hand toward my cart of books. "I'll end class a few minutes early so that you have time to make your first selections. If you have questions my office hours are Thursday afternoons. Feel free to email me at any time, and please direct questions of procedure to Josie. Thank you! See you all at our next lecture."

Chairs scrape back from the table and students head toward my book cart. I wish I could just slip out of the room, but Prof. Sarky would find it odd. I'm supposed to stick around and collect the left-over books.

I can't make such a poor impression on the first day. So I make myself very busy reading the syllabus as people move about the room.

When I look up, Pepe is standing in front of me, three paperbacks in his hand. "Hello *Jhosephine*."

CHAPTER 7
JANUARY

"HELLO, *JHOSEPHINE*."

The back of my neck tingles. My whole life I'd thought I had a boy's name. I was used to hearing, "Hey Jo!" But Pepe makes me sound beautiful every time he says it. If only I believed him.

I lift my chin and find his unhappy face waiting for me. "Hello."

"You have two jobs? That is a lot of working."

"Um, no." I'm not expecting the question, and I stammer out my answer. "I, uh, won't be working at the help center this semester. Only here. For Professor Sarky."

A furrow develops between his big, furry eyebrows. Pepe is a furry guy. *Everywhere.* Just remembering that makes my heart skitter. "You will not be tutoring this term?"

Slowly, I shake my head.

"For anyone?" he clarifies.

Blushing, I nod.

"I see." He doesn't look happy *at all*. "I guess I shall have to find someone else who will put up with all my errors." At that, he gives me a curt nod and leaves the room.

For a second I just stand there feeling shocked. The right comeback takes too long to deliver itself into my brain. *Should have thought about that before ignoring my text, asshole!*

Ten minutes later I walk home, feeling blue. But I'm stunned to find Pepe waiting for me outside my entryway door, hands jammed into his pockets. I pull up short, my keys in my hand. "What's the matter? Forget something?" The words sound bitter, damn it. I'd rather not bleed so profusely in front of him.

"*Salut*," he says, his voice low. "I just need to know one thing."

Why yes, I thought it was more than a one night stand. "Okay?"

"Did you even read my notes?"

"Notes? In class?"

He shakes his head, and his dark eyes have lost their easy warmth. "*Noh*. In your book. The thesaurus."

"In my thesaurus?" I echo stupidly.

There's a flicker of light in his eyes that wasn't there a moment ago. "Yes, *chaton*. Inside. There are sticky notes. I did not want to write in your father's book."

"Sticky notes," I parrot, my keys still in my hand.

He grabs the keys and opens the doors. "Get the book, *chaton*. Please. Where is it?"

I follow him inside, and he hands me the keys so I can open my room door. I walk over to my desk where I'd tossed the offending thesaurus on the morning I left town. Now I pick it up and wipe dust off the cover. Inside I find a sticky note on the very first page.

Chaton—last night was amazing, and I will miss you terribly. I'm sorry I have to dash to Quebec now. That was not good planning. As I have already suspended my USA phone service until January here is my Canada number…

"Oh," I say loudly.

When I turn around, Pepe is leaning against my door, a hand over his eyes. "I am sorry. I wanted to make a nice gesture but I did not guess you would not find it."

"Oh, shit." A half-laugh, half-sob leaps out of my chest.

"So sorry."

"No *I'm* sorry. I thought…" Swallowing is difficult. "It's just…I texted you. And got no answer."

He winces. "I shut it down whenever I'm in Canada, to save a hundred bucks. It goes back on in three days. Would have been worth the cash to avoid this misunderstanding."

An errant tear escapes from one of my eyes and I flick it away, hoping he won't see it.

Too late. "Oh, no!" He crosses my little room in two strides and cups my face in two hands. "Don't be sad." He kisses my cheekbone where the tear landed, and then the other one, too. Then he wraps his arms around me. "Not sad, okay? This semester we are not sad."

"Okay." I take a deep, shaky breath of his woodsy scent. "That was…stupid. I just saw the book on my doorstep and I thought…" I can't even say it aloud. I thought it was such a forgettable night for him that he couldn't get away fast enough.

"I am sorry, too. What a silly thing. I thought maybe you regret me afterwards."

Me? What a crazy idea. "Never," I whisper. To think that Pepe-- Mr. Confidence--would think I didn't want to see him again. And that it would hurt his feelings, too. But this sort of misunderstanding isn't possible unless both people are vulnerable. Maybe awkwardness and insecurity aren't just for me, after all? That's something to think about later. "We should start over."

"Oui."

"Rip up the rough draft and start fresh."

He hums against my forehead, kissing me slowly there. The sensation of his lips against my face is so good that it makes my eyes burn. "No—Let us not edit out the part on your bed. Or drinking wine with pizza. It was all very nice up until the last part."

"True," I say, nuzzling against his cheek. "You're in charge of revisions."

His hand skims down my back, cupping my butt. He gives me a little squeeze. It feels so good I bite my own lip. "I want to start now." His naughty hand lifts the hem of my jacket and circles at my lower back. "But I have class in fifteen minutes."

"Me too."

"We could skip," he says softly, and he dips his head to kiss my neck.

"Skip…the first class of the semester?" my inner nerd girl protests.

"Noh?" He laughs, and I feel the low vibration in my chest. "Ah, well. I have a team dinner after practice. But then may I visit you?"

"Absolutely."

Pepe sighs into my hair. "I waited three weeks to see you again. I suppose I can wait another few hours."

"We should go to class," I say. But then I don't step back.

"We should," he agrees. But then he kisses me.

Five more minutes are lost as Pepe reacquaints himself with my eager mouth. The slide of his tongue against mine is the most distracting thing I've ever known. Harkness College could burn to the ground around us and I don't think I'd notice.

And I'm not sure I'd care.

At long last he steps back, his face flushed, his eyelids heavy. "I think I just made the day even longer. I need to walk you out before I forget how."

Yowza.

The thesaurus is still clutched in my hand. I step back and tuck the book into my backpack.

"There are more notes in there," he says. "I wanted you to have to flip the pages and find them all."

"That is…" I hesitate, because I'm not used to saying freely what I think of him. "…The sweetest thing a guy has ever done for me. Thank you." I hold my door open and he follows me out of the building.

"You can tell me if the grammar is bad. Just don't tell me if they are cheesy." He takes my hand as we walk across the courtyard toward the gate.

"There is no chance I'll think they're cheesy," I say, my face flaming. "Not if you wrote them." He makes a happy noise. I can hardly believe we're holding hands. "Are you really going to take the romance novel class?" I blurt out.

"*Bien sur!* Why not?"

"Didn't think it was your style."

He shrugs, smiling at me. "There is a very cute girl I know who recommends the class. And I get English credits for books that aren't so hard. I can't do Chaucer, *chaton.* My favorite tutor quit."

I give him an eye roll. "I'll still read for you."

"Really?" His face lights up, and he hitches his backpack up on his shoulder. "I think I'll like the romance books, anyway. One of the books has a hockey player on the cover. Hockey in romance books? Is that a thing?"

"It's a thing," I say, blushing. And now I'm embarrassed because…

"Chaton? Did you choose the books for the cart?"

"Um…" Lying seems like a bad idea. But I'm so tempted. "I chose them," I admit. "I chose a wide selection of books which is representative of modern romance. You can check the hockey book for accuracy."

He gives me a sidelong glance, and his smile is knowing. "I took the hockey book. We will look at it together." He squeezes my hand.

"I'm free then," I mutter and he chuckles.

We part ways on College Street, and I get one more kiss for the road. "*Au revoir, chaton*. But not for long."

I walk away.

"Wait!" He bounds after me and pulls a pen from his pack. "My email. So you can reach me before the phone is back." He writes pepe.j.gerault@harkness.edu on my hand.

"What is the J for?" I ask.

"Julien. Write me so I have yours." I get a peck on the lips and then he's gone.

I have to sprint to my history class, and I'm five minutes late. At least it's a huge room, and I can sink into a seat in the back row. I've walked in during the professor's opening remarks, just as Pepe did in Professor Sarky's class. I pull out a notebook, but also the thesaurus.

My bad girl streak is a mile wide today, because I read the rest of Pepe's notes instead of listening to the professor. Pepe has written:

Writing is not my skill, and it's four in the morning. So this could be rough. But you have read all my writing before, and while you always find the errors, you never judge me. I like you so much, chaton. I can't wait to see you again soon. Until then, there are a few more notes in this book, just for you. ~P.

I want to beat my forehead into the little half-desk attached to my lecture hall seat. All that anguish for nothing.

Flipping through the book, I find a sticky note on the page containing "cat." There's a smily face beside an arrow pointing to "kitten" and a devilish smily face under "pussy." But the other notes are sweet. On the page for "beauty" he notes, "all these words remind me of you. I will study them for using later." On the page for "intelligent," he writes, "this page is dedicated to Josephine Allister. I notice there is no page for 'dumb jock.' Maybe in the next edition."

But my favorite note is on the page for "fear." There's an arrow pointing to its synonym, "timidity." Pepe writes, "I was wrong to call you timid. I was the timid one. I like you since last year, but I worry that a smart girl doesn't think much of me. I should send Marie a note of thanks for pushing me in the right direction."

Right then I vow to stop being tongue-tied. I will tell Pepe how I feel, even if it only comes out sounding half as good as the things he says to me. Not one word of this new history class has made it into my brain, and I don't even care. I pull my laptop out and surreptitiously email him. *Thank you for these notes. They are perfect.*

He responds to my message right away. *They are all true, chaton. I am reading the hockey book now.*

Any good?

It's giving me ideas.

Really? For hockey?

No. The hockey is shit. Other parts are better.

???

There are naked parts. :) I will show you later. Might need your dictionary, though.

The Chaucer one?

Whichever one explains "his pulsing member."

My gulp of laughter takes me by surprise, and I do a poor job turning it into a cough. It's unlike me to start a semester by disrupting a class or arriving late. And it's unlike me to plan a tryst for later tonight in my room.

Yet it's already the best semester ever.

CHAPTER 8
L'EPILOGUE

MARCH IS SUPPOSED to be a miserable, rainy month in Harkness, Connecticut. And it's true about the weather. But there's nothing miserable at all about being Pepe's girlfriend.

It's Friday night, and we just beat Harvard in a conference semifinal. I have never been so excited in my life as I was when the buzzer sounded. Down on the ice, the whole team piled onto each other like a pack of puppies, while those poor souls in the Crimson jerseys hung their heads.

"So long, suckers!" I screamed.

Now we're at Capri's which is crammed with an entire ecstatic hockey team and way too many happy fans.

But these days, Nadia and I are no longer lurking in the next room. Tonight I'm tucked into a booth beside Pepe, his arm slung casually around my shoulders as he relives the winning play with John Rikker.

"That deke!" Pepe's low, gravely laughter resonates through my body. I should be listening to the story, but I'm too focused on what will happen a little later tonight. Nadia is out of town, for starters. But earlier this week she made sure to inform Pepe that my birthday is tomorrow, and that she wouldn't be home tonight.

"Magnifique!" he'd said. "At midnight we *celebrate*."

At the time I'd been embarrassed at this little exchange. But now?

Not so much. Every time Pepe touches me tonight, I check the clock, but midnight just won't hurry.

I'm like Cinderella in reverse, waiting for the clock to strike. I can't wait to shed a slipper…and then all the rest of my clothing.

But first, hockey smack talk.

"Did you see the look on their goalie's face?" Rikker asks, and then cackles. "Trevi snuck in there and that dude was *not* expecting it."

"Boom!" Pepe shouts. "He put the cookie in the…" My boyfriend stops, frowning.

"The biscuit in the basket?" Rikker asks, grinning.

"What is a biscuit in English?" Pepe asks.

"In America it's a buttery thing, but not sweet," I explain.

"Although in the UK, a biscuit *is* a cookie," Rikker adds.

Pepe buries his face in his hands. "I will never get English."

"But you get hockey, and we're headed to the finals!" Rikker holds up a hand, which I high five. "Lake Placid, baby! It's going to be awesome."

I sneak a look at my watch. It's after eleven-thirty. Not long now.

"You want anything from the bar?" Rikker asks. "I'm getting a pitcher."

Pepe slaps a ten on the table. "Can you bring *Jhosephine* a glass of wine?"

"Of course." Rikker nudges the ten away. "But I hear she's having a birthday. It's on me."

"Thanks," I say. "That's so nice." But inside I'm thinking, *who needs another glass of wine? We could just go home and jump each other*.

Lately our tutoring sessions are going really well. And I'm not talking about essay writing.

Pepe's hand curls around the side of my body as Rikker walks away. "It is almost time for your birthday surprise," he says right into my ear. "I can't wait."

"Me neither," I admit. I turn my head and kiss him. PDA is so not like me. But the man is seriously attractive, and when he whispers in my ear I go a little crazy sometimes.

Pepe kisses me slowly and then pulls away, his dark eyes glittering. "You need to press pause on that, *chaton*. Just a little while longer."

"Why?" I whine. "We could just leave now."

He closes his eyes and gives his head a quick shake. Then he opens them again. "How did I get so lucky?"

"What do you mean?"

"Some girls—they only want the bling and the jersey and the front row seats to the conference final. You just want to drag me home and kiss me."

"Well of course I do."

His eyes gleam. "*Désolé*. You have to wait ten minutes because I make a surprise for you that happens here."

Rikker sets a glass of wine in front of me. "Pepe, Bella is looking for you." He points at the doorway.

My heart sinks just a little bit. Lately I've worked out that Bella and Pepe used to fool around sometimes, during those intervals when Marie had broken up with Pepe. They never mention it, but I've heard a joke or two these last couple of months.

So I usually avoid Bella, because I don't like thinking about the two of them together.

We both look toward the entrance, and sure enough, Bella is standing there, the bar lighting making a perfect halo of her shimmering blond curls. It doesn't help my confidence that she's ridiculously beautiful.

Pepe raises a hand and gives her a thumb's up sign. Then Bella smiles and disappears.

I don't know what that's all about. But then suddenly I do. Bella reappears, this time lit up by candle light. And those candles are on a cake…

John Rikker grabs a spoon and taps his glass to get everyone's attention. "Listen up! Somebody else has to start the singing Happy Birthday to Josie because you do not want it to be me," he says.

"*Happy Birthday to you!*" Sings a younger player named D.J. He's a substitute on the team, although tonight he scored his first goal of the season. And apparently he and his girlfriend can both sing, because together they carry the song for two bars before the whole team joins in.

My birthday has never been so loud.

I just sit there with my mouth hanging open as Bella draws closer. It's a big cake—rectangular but tall. When she finally sets it down in front of me, I can finally make out its shape. It's styled like a *book*. *ROGET'S THESAURUS*, it reads. *EDIBLE EDITION*.

It's the cutest thing I have ever seen in my entire life. And Pepe is grinning and singing a very enthusiastic but slightly off key version of Happy Birthday.

To *me*.

"Oh, wow," I say when the song ends.

"Make a wish!" Rikker yells, holding up his phone to take a picture.

I take a deep breath and blow all the candles out. Okay, it takes two breaths. It's a lot of candles on a big cake.

"*Joyeux Anniversaire!*" Pepe says, squeezing me.

"Here's a knife," Bella says, handing it to me.

"Thank you. Both of you," I say, including Bella.

She shrugs. "Pepe did the whole thing. I just took delivery at the front door."

"Let's eat it," Pepe suggests.

So I cut the cake and Bella produces a stack of little paper plates. After I serve a bunch of slices she takes over for me so I can eat one. "Single file line, boys!" she says. "No elbows. Save those for the finals next week."

Pepe eats a huge slice of cake and then teases me when I can barely finish mine. "There is one more thing," he says, reaching for his gym bag on the floor. "I got you a present. It is a little strange…"

"You didn't have to do that," I say quickly. Although I'm pretty excited to see what it is.

He hands me a pink gift bag, and I reach inside. It's a T-shirt. Gray, with pink letters. It reads:

The first rule of thesaurus club is we don't speak, mention, jabber, natter, expound upon, discourse or declare thesaurus club.

"*Oh my God!*" I squeal.

Pepe's grin grows wider. "You like it?"

"I *love* it." *And I love you.* It's too soon to say that. But only the best kind of guy would know how much I adore this T-shirt. Pepe and I have only been together for three months. Okay, not even that long. But he somehow managed to choose a gift that was incredibly meaningful without being too expensive or too intimate. "It's perfect in every way," I assure him.

"Let's see," Bella says, helping herself to a blob of frosting that clings to the cake's tray.

When I turn the shirt around, she cackles. "That is nerdy and cool."

It's tempting to bristle at the nerdy comment, but only because it's Bella that made it. Imagine what I'd be like if I ever met Marie, his long-term girlfriend. One look at her and I'd probably implode with jealousy.

I'm still new at this girlfriend thing. But I've never dated anyone as popular as Pepe before. Last week we were at a party at the hockey house, and I watched a girl actually tuck her phone number into his pocket.

He just laughed it off, of course. But I wanted to smack her.

"Do you want to take extra cake home?" Pepe asks. "Or should I find someone to eat the last slice?"

"Let's find a hockey player to eat it, and then let's get out of here."

"Good call, *Jhosephine*," he says. "One moment."

Pepe picks up the cake and moves across the room to offer it to a friend.

"Happy Birthday," Bella says, gathering up a couple of sticky plates and forks. "He was super excited about that cake. He took a picture of your thesaurus on his phone and showed it to the bakery." She smiles and shakes her head. "Don't worry so much, okay? You don't need to."

Wait, what? "I don't worry," I say quickly.

Bella rolls her eyes. "Right. Sure you don't."

I sigh. "Okay, fine. I do. I just care too much sometimes."

"No," Bella shakes her head. "There is no such thing. Trust me. You and Pepe are the real deal. I know it when I see it. Speaking of which…" She checks her phone. "My man is back from visiting his mom. Gotta run! There's things to see and a boy to do."

These words don't make Bella blush, so I do it for her. It will be a good long time before I can talk about sex without turning red-faced. "Goodnight. And thanks for helping with my birthday cake."

She winks at me on the way out.

Pepe comes back. "Ready, *chaton?*"

I slide out of the booth and put on my jacket, tucking my gift back into its bag and hooking it over my hand. Pepe shoulders his gym bag, and we walk out into the night together. This is the same walk we did that evening in December, when I didn't know how to invite him up to my room.

I'll never be smooth, but I'm getting a little better at saying what I want. "Can I ask you a question?"

"*Bien sûr.*"

"Do you ever miss Marie? It's okay if you do."

Pepe turns his head sharply, his expression startled. "Noh? I don't think about her much."

"But you were together for such a long time."

He shrugs. "Yes, and letting go was hard. But now that I have, it's better. We outgrow each other, Marie and I. She called me last week and…"

"Last week?" I blurt out.

"*Oui.* She wants to see me over spring break."

My heart staggers around in my chest.

"I tell her no. And it was so easy! I don't want to play games. You never do that. You say you're not so good at talking, but I don't know if it's true. Some people say too much, no? Marie always wanted me to know how unhappy she was when I went away. Like coming to Harkness was something I was doing to her intentionally. Like a punishment."

"That's not fair," I say, even though it isn't really my place to weigh in.

He shrugs. "I am happier now. You and I have fun, and we're kind to each other." His dark eyes find mine, and they're shiny in the lamplight. "It's not so complicated, I think. To be with you."

We've arrived at the gate to Fresh Court. "You're coming home with me, right?" I say. The words just tumble right out, with no hesitation.

"Of course, *chaton*. For as long as you'll have me."

He squeezes my hand, and we cross the slate path toward Parker. I lead him up the steps and put my key in the lock.

Pepe leans in to kiss my neck, and my fingers pause on the key. "I like that so much," I whisper.

"Yes? And do you also like this?" He leans in and kisses my ear, then draws my earlobe into his mouth.

Goosebumps break out all over my body. "Yes. Very much."

"Open that door, *chaton*. There are many other questions I have for you in this matter."

I open the door and hurry through the hallway, opening my room, too.

Once inside, I don't turn on the light.

Pepe takes the hint. He takes the gift bag from my hand and tosses both our bags onto my desk. Then he eases my jacket off my shoulders and kisses me. "Happy Birthday, *chaton*. I'm going to make it even happier."

I know he will, and I can't wait.

THE
END

YESTERDAY

IT'S BEEN ALMOST SEVEN YEARS SINCE JOHN RIKKER LEFT MICHIGAN.

That ought to be long enough to scar over all the wounds the place left on him. Shouldn't it?

When Rikker returns to the scene of the crime, he finds surviving a week with his parents to be harder than he'd guessed.

And Graham can't stand by and let him handle it alone…

CHAPTER 1
RIKKER

YOUR RESERVATION NUMBER IS 87XTY442.

I close my laptop and grab my phone. Then I jog down the stairs of my grandmother's house and out the front door, because it's a beautiful day for December, and the cell phone reception is always better outside.

Gran is sitting in a rocker on the porch with a down comforter over her lap, reading glasses perched on her nose, and a paperback mystery novel in her good hand. She glances up as I fly past. "Where's the fire?"

"Sorry." I chuckle, skidding to a halt. "Just made my travel arrangements for the day after Christmas, and I'm going to call Graham and tell him."

She gives me a nod. "You tell that hunk hello for me."

"I will."

"And when you're off the phone, it will be time for cookies and hot chocolate."

"It's always time for cookies and hot chocolate. Back in five, and I'll grab it for us."

Smiling, she goes back to her book.

These days, the cookies we eat come from the bakery in town. Gran's dexterity isn't what it used to be, and she doesn't bake very often anymore. The stroke she suffered eight months ago has slowed her down some.

Still, after months of therapy, she's recovered much of her independence. Last summer I hadn't wanted to leave her alone for any amount of time, but now she's doing much better.

I walk a few paces down the driveway and touch Graham's number on my phone. "Hey, babe," I say when he picks up.

"Hey."

That's his standard greeting when we speak on the phone. But his voice is husky, and I don't need more than that one word to know how badly he misses me. His "hey" is weighty, conveying the gravity of the situation: we haven't seen each other since winter break started a week ago.

But relief is on the horizon. "I just bought a plane ticket," I tell him.

"Yeah?" That's Grahamspeak for *hot damn*. My boyfriend is understated, but I love him anyway.

"Sure did. I'm flying into Grand Rapids on Sunday. Flying out of Chicago the following Sunday."

"How much of that time do I get?"

"That all depends on whether you're coming to Chicago with me. I can bring a plus-one to this wedding. You won't have to wear a suit, either. Just a jacket." *Please come with me*, I privately beg.

There's a beat of silence on his end. "You sure I won't be in the way?"

"Not a chance. Does that mean you'll come?"

"Of course I will."

"Yeah?" I grin like an idiot. "Full disclosure—Skippy's wedding will probably feature sequins and glitter and cheesy music."

"Whatever, I don't care," he says firmly. "There'll be a hotel room in Chicago, right?"

"Hell yes."

"That's plenty of incentive."

"Good point," I say lightly. If Graham is willing to accompany me to my ex-boyfriend's wedding, this whole trip just became a lot more fun.

"Can I pick you up at the airport on Sunday?" Graham asks.

"I was hoping you would. My flight arrives a few minutes before noon."

"Your parents will still be at church, anyway."

"Yeah, I did that on purpose." My visit to Michigan has been scheduled to conveniently sidestep Sunday morning. "I just couldn't see myself walking in that church with them, pretending I'm not still pissed off at the pastor for *counseling* my mother all these years. I can't shake that man's hand and make nice."

Graham makes a low noise of disgust. "You don't have to visit your parents at all, you know. Come to Michigan and stay with us the whole time."

"I wish. But my dad's been campaigning for this visit since April. I blew him off over the summer. And it's just a few days, right? I can grit my teeth for that long."

"Shouldn't have to grit 'em at all," Graham points out. "But when it's over, I'll give you a reward for your patience."

"Yeah? Tell me more."

"Can't right now," he mutters. I hear voices in the background. "Call me tonight."

"You can bet on it. Miss you."

"Back atcha, hottie."

I hang up smiling. Graham will be my reward for suffering through a few days with my parents. He's my happy thought.

CHAPTER 2
RIKKER

AS THE JET descends over snowy Western Michigan corn fields, I'm not smiling anymore. This is the first time I've been here in almost seven years, and I don't feel ready to face this place again.

Too bad I didn't figure that out before I got on this plane.

I hadn't left Michigan on my own accord. But I thought by now I might be finished feeling angry about it. As the jet touches down at the airport, I realize I'm not over it. Not by a long shot.

It's going to be a long couple of days.

The familiar *ding* alerts passengers that the *Fasten Seatbelt* sign has been turned off. People stir in their seats and open the overhead bins.

This is it. I'm back in the town that once spat me out, and it's hard to care about seeing it again.

"Excuse me," whispers the middle-aged woman beside me. Until I get up, she's trapped on the plane.

That gets me moving. I heave my carcass out of the seat and pull my carryon suitcase out of the overhead compartment. A line of people begins shuffling off the plane ahead of me.

Six years ago I'd left Michigan with cracked ribs and my arm in a sling. I'd been attacked by a few rednecks in an alley, because they'd seen Graham and I kissing in a car. The injuries sent me to the hospital, where I'd been foolish enough to tell my parents the truth about what happened to me.

But my worst scars are the kind you can't see. After I was released from the hospital, my parents drove me to my grandmother's place in Vermont so I could "heal from my injuries." The trouble is they never came back. I spent the rest of high school living with Gran, because my parents couldn't stomach having a gay son.

Vermont is my home now, and I love it there. Michigan is just a sore spot, and always will be.

I never should have agreed to this.

For the past few years, my parents and I have had a polite relationship based on greeting cards and the occasional short phone call. Right after Gran's stroke was the first time I'd seen them in years. That had only been for a couple of minutes. And it didn't go that well.

But my dad had begged me to come home for a little family visit. So here I am. Following all the other passengers, I get off the plane and walk through the terminal for the first time since I was sixteen.

Weirdly, everything looks exactly the same, down to the blue carpet and the sparse count of gates. Beyond security, I see the same old Starbucks on the left-hand side. And all around me I hear the flattened-vowel sounds of the Midwest.

It's trippy. Like I've time-traveled.

"Rik!"

The universe snaps back into focus when I hear my boyfriend call my name. And there's Graham, jogging toward me, a big smile on his face.

Damn. That smile makes me so fucking happy. And so does the rest of the picture—wide shoulders, long legs. He's wearing a V-neck sweater over a dress shirt, and a pair of khakis. He probably left church early to pick me up. The shirt is open at the collar, and my hungry gaze gets stuck on the V of smooth, golden skin on his chest. I wanted to put my mouth right there. And then unbutton the shirt a little farther…

But as he closes in, it occurs to me to wonder what the next two seconds will bring. More smiles and a slap on the back?

A kiss? No—not that. My Graham does not do PDA.

The mystery is solved when Graham steps in close and pulls me into a tight hug. Seriously, my ribs are compromised by two very strong arms squeezing me. It doesn't last long, but the hug is accompanied by a happy sigh. "Missed you," he whispers before releasing me.

I just stand there like a dope for a moment, taking him in. Graham's skin is a warm color even in the winter. Those cool blue eyes study me, and I start to grin. "If I have to come to fucking *Michigan*, at least I get to look at you."

His smile fades. "You get to look at me *some*. But I have some bad news."

"Yeah?" My stomach drops.

He sighs. "Today my mom called your house and asked if your family could come over for dinner tomorrow or the next night. But your mother, uh, declined. She said she was keeping you busy with family things, because they haven't seen you in so long."

"Wait. Is that the bad news?"

He frowns. "Yeah."

I laugh out loud. "Shit, G. I thought you were going to cancel our trip to Chicago."

He puts a hand on my back, steering me down the ramp toward the baggage claim. "Hell no. But the weekend is *days* from now. I thought you'd be over for dinner tomorrow, or at least out with me somewhere. And now it sounds like she's going to hold you hostage. You have luggage?"

"Just the carryon. I travel light in case I have to make a quick getaway."

I'd meant it as a joke, but Graham winces. "You know that you can call me any time, right? If this visit isn't working for you, just send me a text and I'll pick you up."

"Thanks." He will, too. And what's more, his parents would be happy to see me. When Graham finally came out to his mother in the spring, she hugged him while he cried.

My parents? *They* cried, and then began reading literature about conversion camps.

But my grandmother told them, "Just bring him to me. He's going to love Vermont."

Thank God for Gran. She's my real family now. She's the one I'd brought my high school boyfriend home to meet. She helped me pick out my tux before prom. She and I watch *Game of Thrones* together, rating the men on a scale of one to ten. (Gran has a thing for Jorah.)

And the so-called parents I'm a half hour away from seeing? I have no idea how this awkward little adventure will go. Anything could happen. My stomach does a dip and roll as I follow Graham down the familiar corridor, past the baggage claim, and toward the glass doors to the outside. But then I halt in surprise. "Where did that come from?"

"What?" Graham turns around.

I point at the structure looming in front of us. "There didn't used to be a parking garage here. It was just a lot before."

"Sure..." My boyfriend's forehead crinkles as he studies me. "They built this because it snows so much. Everyone's car was buried when they flew back after that Florida vacation."

"Oh," I say, my blood pressure inexplicably elevated. Normally, I don't give a crap about parking garages. And even though the sameness inside the airport made me feel crazy, the differentness outside is almost worse.

This place makes me feel off-balance, like the earth has shifted under my feet. I just want to go home where nobody will judge me.

Fuck you, Michigan. The whole mitten state can kiss my big gay ass.

Graham reaches out to squeeze my elbow. "Come on," he says softly. "My mom's car is on the first level."

Unfortunately, Grand Rapids is a small enough town that it only takes Graham a half hour to drive me home, including hitting the drive-through at a Starbucks and then talking in the car for ten minutes together.

"Did you rent a car for Chicago? If you didn't have time, I'll do it." I sip my cappuccino while holding Graham's hand with my free one.

His thumb strokes my palm. "Yeah. Did it right away. Did you write your toast yet?"

"Not exactly. But how hard could it be? I'm going to tell a couple of funny snowboarding stories." *Shit.* That sounds dumb. "My toast is going to suck. But I'll make it short."

"It won't suck. Tell 'em how Skippy taught you to snowboard because he saw that the flatlander needed help."

I'd forgotten about that. "Not bad, G. You want to write this thing? You're the journalist. Please? I'll make it worth your while."

He snickers. "You sit with it a while longer. I'll read it for you when you think it's done."

"All right."

"Are you ready?" he asks me, and suddenly we're talking about my folks' place again.

"I guess."

"Your dad's been after you to visit a while now," he points out. "He wouldn't invite you here to make you miserable."

I consider that. It's true that Dad had wanted me to visit over the summer. But I hadn't done it. Graham had come to Vermont for the summer instead.

Those were nice months. Since Gran had relocated to the main floor of the farmhouse, where it was easier for her to move around, Graham and I had the whole second floor to ourselves. We worked some daytime shifts at a farm stand nearby and spent our nights having very quiet sex on the twin beds we'd lassoed together to make a king-sized space.

Best summer ever.

But Dad had kept at me to come to Michigan. And this after several years where he'd seemed to forget I exist? Gran put him up to it, I think. That traitor.

So here I sit.

"I'll survive it," I grumble. Dropping my coffee cup into the holder, I reach for Graham.

In spite of our frightening history of car-kisses in Michigan, he doesn't even check to see if anyone might be watching. He leans in, his cool eyes locked on mine. Then they flip shut as we connect properly for the first time in way too long. The first kiss is slow and loaded with too much tension. *Parents. The holidays. Tuxes. A speech.*

"Baby," I whisper against his lips. I cup his face in one hand, and his smooth jaw is so achingly familiar that I begin to relax. I touch my tongue to the seam of his lips, and he opens on a sigh.

The next kiss is deep and slow for all the right reasons. The slide of his tongue against mine is everything I need. My fingers find their way onto his sturdy chest, and our teeth click as we try to make it linger.

But we're in the cramped front seat of a Subaru, and I'm due at the parents' place now. Reluctantly, I ease back, breaking the kiss with a groan of frustration. "That will have to tide me over."

He grunts with unhappiness and sits back in his seat. Then he turns the key and starts the engine, and I try not to imagine that Graham is driving me toward my doom.

CHAPTER 3
GRAHAM

DROPPING Rikker off in front of his parents' house feels awful.

"Want me to come in with you?" I offer. His mother hates my guts, but I don't give a damn about that. I'll go inside if he wants me there.

But he shakes his head. "I'll call you later."

I don't get a kiss goodbye. He opens the door, shoulders his bag, and walks toward the house. The front door opens when he reaches it, and I see him disappear inside.

Feeling glum, I drive the few short blocks home.

My parents are in the kitchen, eating take-out burgers. "Sit!" my mother insists. "We brought you something for lunch."

"Thanks," I say, dropping into a chair and pulling the bag toward me.

"How is he?" my mom asks, dipping a french fry in ketchup.

"Unexcited. But fine, I guess." I unwrap the sandwich and take a grateful bite.

"He's welcome here anytime," my father says. "Can't believe they won't join us for dinner tomorrow."

"Or ever," I grunt.

"How Christian of them," my father says, the comment dripping with irony.

"They're Christian, unless you're gay," I add, supplying Mrs. Rikker's outlook on life.

My mother sighs. "Not everyone thinks like that."

"I know." The church my parents attend these days has a rainbow banner on the wall of the lobby.

They actually had to switch churches after I came out during my junior year of college. My mom had assumed their former congregation was more open-minded than the Rikkers' church. But when my mother told her pastor about my struggle to accept myself, his reaction wasn't positive enough for her.

She's become my fiercest advocate. So, after almost thirty years in their congregation, my parents walked out the door, visiting a new church the following Sunday. And they've never looked back.

I felt bad about it at the time. But being out has been so much better than being in the closet. I finally understand that. I wish there hadn't been any collateral damage, but we're all adjusting well enough now.

Two years ago it wouldn't have occurred to me that I could sit here at the kitchen table with my folks, eating burgers, having a casual conversation about my boyfriend's asshat parents.

"I love you guys," I say quietly. Saying things like that hasn't always been my style. But Rikker has turned me into someone who can express himself, at least once in a while.

"Aw, Mikey," my mother says, rubbing my arm. "Why do you look so blue?"

"I'm not," I lie. "I have some good news, by the way. Just checked my school email account and found a job interview request."

"Yessss!" My father pumps his fist. "Where is it?"

"Washington, D.C., for Sports Night TV."

"This is great!" my mother cheers. "When will you meet them?"

"Next month."

"Let's go suit shopping tomorrow," my mother suggests. "You need to look sharp."

"All right. Thanks."

Finding a post-college job has proven harder than I'd thought it would be. The process isn't exactly an ego boost. I've sent a staggering number of resumes out, and received only a handful of calls from news outlets. If I don't find something soon, I'll have to take a job that's not as interesting to me or graduate jobless.

Last year I was terrified to be gay. I got over that only to find myself terrified of being unemployed.

And if that isn't scary enough, I can't stand peering into the dark, hollow place in my soul that's afraid of being separated from Rikker. What if he gets tired of waiting for me? Long distance will be a drag, and my boyfriend has a high sex drive.

Ugh. I'm going to spend the whole next semester worrying about this, I just know it. And before that, I'm going to spend the next three days worrying about Rikker and how he might be getting along with his bitchy mother.

After lunch I volunteer to help my dad clean out the garage. He's overjoyed to have help with this chore, and I need something to keep my hands busy. I keep checking my phone, hoping for updates from Rikker. I'm uneasy about his stay with his parents. If they weren't willing to acknowledge our relationship, what does that mean for his time in their home? Are they going to lecture him? If they do, will he just sit there and take it? Or will he explode from frustration?

I'd left him on their doorstep, and I'm not sure I should have. Sure, Rik is an adult who can take care of himself. But hell if I don't want to punch anyone who is mean to him.

These are my uneasy thoughts as I help my father sort his old tools and hang them on pegs above the workbench. When we're finished, I take a hot shower and check my phone. Again.

There's a new text message, only it isn't from Rikker. It's a group text including six of my hockey teammates from high school. *MINI REUNION!* it shouts. *Founders Brewery, Tuesday, 5p. Who can make it?*

I hesitate.

Since I spent last summer in Vermont, I haven't seen my high school teammates for a long time—not since the summer before junior year. In other words, I haven't seen them since before I began dating a dude, and before I came out to my family.

Before acknowledging my sexuality, I spent years drowning my frustrations in women and whiskey. All my high school friends knew *that* Michael Graham.

Now I'm done being a coward. Rikker convinced me that it feels better knowing which people are true friends. Coming out makes that all very clear. At Harkness I've been gratified (and in some cases stunned) to learn that most everyone accepts the real me. And the rejection of a few people who weren't all that great to begin with hasn't sunk me.

On the other hand, do I have the energy right now to put myself out there to all of those old friends?

After thinking about it for a few minutes, I respond with: *I'm in. See you Tuesday.*

Tuesday is still two days before I'm supposed to see Rikker again. Beer and hockey smack talk will get my mind off a few things. I'll be climbing the walls in the meantime.

After dinner with my folks, I get into bed with the TV remote. But it's just an excuse to keep one eye on my phone. Finally, at ten, I text Rik again, because I can't help myself.

Graham: *Dude. I've been checking my phone all day like a desperate loser. It's not that I expect phone sex tonight. But just let me know you're okay.*

To my great relief, he begins to respond right away.

Rikker: *Sorry! My dad took me to a Griffins game this afternoon, and I left my phone behind because I was trying to be a good son.*

Graham: *How was the game?*

Rikker: *Fine. It's weird to watch an AHL game and wonder if I can get there.*

Graham: *You will! And how was the conversation?*

Rikker: *Fine. But I didn't test my dad. We were both really fucking polite.*

Graham: *You didn't point out the most lickable players, and rate them on a scale of 1-10?*

Rikker: *Why bother? You're hotter than the whole team. Times ten.*

Graham: *Baby, you don't have to butter me up. I'll give you whatever you want. I'm free right this second. And I'm less than a mile away.*

Rikker: *Which is too far. But only for another couple days. My old room is smaller than I remember it.*

Graham: *Being there must be weird AF.*

Rikker: *Yup. My old hockey medals are hanging here. Mom must dust them. So it's like a shrine to being 16.*

Graham: *How is it going with her?*

Rikker: *OK. Awkward. We're all trying not to say the wrong thing.*

Graham: *Sounds like a blast.*

Rikker: *Pretty much. Mom made my favorite dinner—chicken parm. I'm taking that as a good sign?*

Graham: *Can I come and pick you up tomorrow afternoon? We could go to a movie. Or anywhere at all.*

Rikker: *Nothing would make me happier. But I'm going to play the good son and hang here. It's only a few days, right? And maybe my mother will relax if I don't rush for the exits.*

Graham: *Why does she deserve coddling, though? I want to just drive over there and make her look me in the eye.*

Rikker: *You are 100% right. But I'm doing this for my dad, because he's trying to build a bridge over the crevasse. He made the effort, so I'm trying.*

Graham: *You're a better man than I.*

Rikker: *I love you anyway. :)*

Graham: *Just for that, you get another blow job on Thursday night. DO YOU HEAR THAT, MRS R? I'M GOING TO SUCK ON YOUR SON'S PENIS. HE LIKES IT.*

Rikker: *LOL. You've come a long way, baby.*

Graham: *And yet here I sit alone.*

Rikker: *I'm all yours on Thursday.*

Graham: *I know. And I don't want to give you guilt. Just miss you.*

Rikker: *Good night, cutie.*

Graham: *Night. :)*

CHAPTER 4
RIKKER

ON MY SECOND day in Michigan, the hours go by at a crawl.

I accompany my mother to see the Christmas display at the sculpture garden. The *sculpture garden!* Kill me already. I'm the youngest person there by about forty years.

Afterward, my mother announces that she has to attend a meeting at church. Some women's club thing. And my dad doesn't get home from work for another hour and a half.

Home alone, I text Graham quickly, asking him what he's up to.

He doesn't answer for an hour, though, because he's gone shopping with his mom and then downtown to meet his father for a late lunch. And when he finally replies, I can't even bear to tell him that I'd meant to walk over to see him.

The missed opportunity grates on me, so it would probably drive him nuts.

Later, I sit through another stilted meal with my parents, my mother's sister Janet, and her nearly mute husband. It gets awkward when Aunt Janet asks me The Question. "Have you met any nice girls at school that I should know about?"

The moment the question leaves her lips, my mother's hand freezes on her water glass. The silence hangs between us, ready to choke us all, while my father stares at his scalloped potatoes. He seems to be holding his breath.

"Uh, I guess I haven't," I say, shoving another bite of pot roast in my mouth.

Then? I have the worst urge to *laugh*.

Why am I playing this role? I feel like I'm living inside one of the less successful SNL skits. My mother obviously doesn't discuss my sexual orientation even with her closest sister. I'm *that* shameful in her eyes.

I'm this close to stopping our polite little meal by putting down my fork and announcing, "Actually, I have a *boyfriend*."

But if I do that, a shouting match will be the likely result. And my visit with the parents will come to a quick end. Part of me craves the conflict. But it will only hurt my dad, and possibly me. The truth is that I can't afford to rock the boat. I need to get through college. I need them to pay the part of my tuition that financial aid doesn't cover.

In a year and a half I'll be truly free.

Making nice is even harder than I'd expected it to be, though. And Graham was right when he said that my mom doesn't deserve me.

Two more days, I promise myself. The silent deal we've struck, if I understand it correctly, is that they'll pay for school and pretend to have a busy son on the East Coast as long as I help them pretend I'm not a disgrace.

It's not the best deal ever. But neither is it the worst. Eighteen months from now I'll have a Harkness degree and probably a good job, if not a spot on a minor league hockey team. And my parents won't hold any sway over my life ever again.

One thing is certain, though—this will be my last Michigan visit. I can't do this again.

Dad steers the dinnertime conversation to hockey, which is his way of finding a topic that flatters me. He's trying to be diplomatic. I don't really understand why. But he's trying.

I clean my plate and hope that diplomacy is enough to get us through another forty-eight hours.

After my aunt and uncle leave, Dad talks me into watching some TV. There's no hockey game on, sadly. But Dad puts on the last part of some nature series he's been following. I watch a bunch of emperor penguin chicks hatch. They are shockingly cute, with big eyes and a loud chirp.

It's all fun and games until several mother penguins become trapped in this slippery little ice ravine. One of the mothers shuffles out one painstaking inch at a time, her chick on her feet, her beak an ice pick she employs for hours, until victory is reached.

But another penguin mom can't figure it out, and she ends up abandoning her chick. She waddles away, leaving it to shiver and cry by itself.

They don't actually show its dead body, but we all know that's what's coming. Why do people watch this shit? I want to kick the television. By the time I go to bed, I'm full-on depressed. And it doesn't help that bedding down in my old bedroom is a lot like having an out-of-body experience. The light fixture is the same. The bedspread is the same. Blue corduroy.

Seven years.

The old, closeted me had walked out of here on a spring day, sixteen years old, heading for Graham's house. I'd had the car keys, and an idea that I wanted to drive Graham over to a comic book shop in a dodgy section of Grand Rapids.

We didn't make it into the shop that day, because I kissed him before we got out of the car. As we crossed the parking lot, they pounced. *Fucking faggots.* I got the beating of a lifetime, and Graham escaped.

I spent four days in the hospital. Or was it five? How weird that I can no longer remember. After my discharge, I'd come home for maybe twenty-four hours before my dad put me in the car and drove me to Gran's house in Vermont.

My life changed then. I never looked back.

But now I'm forced to. Lying here in my old digs, I'm still angry. I'm mad at the assholes who kicked me until I passed out. I'm mad at my parents for freaking out about their gay kid. And I'm furious at myself for just accepting my banishment like I deserved it.

And for coming back here at all. Who needs this shit?

Deep breaths, I remind myself. *This is stupid, but you can make it.*

I pick up my phone and text Graham. ***Hey! You still up?***

Right here! he replies immediately.

I quickly relax. *I survived the sculpture garden and a nature show on TV*, I tap out. *How was your day?*

Horny, is his quick response. And I laugh.

I dream about that fucking penguin. And the next day passes slowly. I take my parents out to lunch, which isn't so bad. But my dad goes back to work afterwards, leaving my mom and I alone to struggle for conversation in the afternoon.

At five o'clock my mother suggests that I put on a nice shirt for dinner. "I'm making a taco bake," she adds.

I hesitate, trying to follow this logic. As far as I know, faux-Mexican food doesn't require proper attire. "Who am I dressing up for?" I ask. If she's trying to fix me up with a "nice girl" from church, it's going to be a long evening.

"Father VanderBeek is coming over," she says. "He loves my taco bake."

Her pastor.

Shit.

I go into my bedroom and open the closet door. I take out the lone button-down shirt I've brought and slowly put it on. Then I sit down on the familiar bedspread and listen to the bed springs creak in the silence.

Maybe Father VanderBeek comes for dinner a lot. Maybe it's nothing. But I have a bad feeling about this dinner.

I get up and go back to the kitchen. "Mom? Is there any particular topic on the agenda for tonight? Or is this just a friendly visit from the pastor?"

She adjusts the flame under the saucepan of refried beans she's heating. "Of course it's a friendly visit. But he will also minister to our needs while he's here."

"And what needs might those be?" I ask, irritation creeping into the question.

She turns and pins me with a stare. "He wants to talk to you about therapy, John. Just a chat about your options."

"My options," I say slowly. "I don't need options. I'm good the way I am."

She sighs and stirs the beans. "Just hear him out. It's an hour of your time. He only has your best interests at heart. We all do."

My blood pressure spikes, and I turn around and walk out of the kitchen.

Back in the bedroom, I unlock my phone. My hands are actually shaking. *You around?* I text Graham.

No response.

Shit.

I grab my suitcase off the floor and set it on the bed. From the bathroom I retrieve my shaving kit and my toothbrush. Those go into the bag. Then I slip into Mom's laundry room and open the dryer mid-cycle. The two T-shirts I'd thrown in with her load this afternoon are still damp, but I take them out anyway, restarting the dryer afterwards.

As I push the black button, I feel certifiably insane. After all, it's only polite to restart the dryer when you're making your escape from Crazyville.

It takes me about three minutes to pack completely. Then I just sit there on the edge of the bed for a little while longer, checking in with myself about what I'm about to do. Is it worth getting cut off financially by my parents to avoid a really uncomfortable couple of hours with a bigot who believes I'm heading straight for hell?

I take a deep breath and blow it out.

Yeah.

This was never going to work.

On shaking legs, I stand. Then I walk slowly through my parents' little house for the last time. My mother has disappeared, probably into her bedroom to change. So it is without confrontation or ceremony that I let myself out the front door, my bag on my shoulder. The walk to the Grahams' place won't take long at all.

CHAPTER 5
GRAHAM

THE FOUNDERS BREWING COMPANY TAPROOM is a place my friends and I had always yearned to go as teenagers. Now walking in is as easy as handing over my ID.

"Enjoy," the bouncer says.

"Thanks, man." *I'll try. But it's gonna be interesting.*

I glance around the big room, looking for my high school friends. The place is so large that it takes me a minute to spot them at a long table against the far wall.

Maybe it's generosity, or maybe it's nerves, but I count heads and then make a stop at the bar. My first move will be to buy a round of whatever award-winning fancy ale is on special today.

"Can I help you?"

The beer sure can. "Tell me about the special."

The bartender launches into a description of its fruity hops and flavors, but I'm too nervous to listen. At the end of his lengthy recitation I realize I haven't heard a word. "Eight pints of the special, please."

The bartender quotes a surprisingly high price, and I hand him my credit card. Fancy ale does not come cheap, apparently, even in the Midwest.

They give me a tray, which I carefully transport to the table full of hockey players.

"Hey, does anyone recognize that guy?" our old captain crows.

"Yeah, do we know you?" someone adds.

As a matter of fact, you really don't! "Yeah." I clear my throat, setting the tray down on the table. "I'm the guy who just bought you a beer."

"Well, all right," my former teammate Jason says with a smile. "Suppose you can stay."

I settle into a chair beside Jason and sip my overpriced beer. Everyone has a story. And since we're all graduating in the spring, post-college plans are the topic du jour. One guy is headed to California for law school. Another one has taken a job here in town at an investment firm. Someone else is taking the MCATs for a try at med school.

Our team captain, Matty Newman, is getting *married* this winter. Jesus.

"Dude, why?" someone teases. "Is she pregnant?"

Newman shakes his head with a smile. "Just ready to tie the knot. We've been together four years already. We want to live together, and her parents would make a big stink if she just moved in with me."

"Who cares what they think?" I hear myself ask. Heads swivel in my direction, and I regret the outburst. "You seem really happy about it, and that's cool. But I hope making her daddy happy is just an added benny, not the only reason to get hitched."

Newman's fingers worry the edges of the coaster under his beer. "It makes *Lisa* happy. She really wants out of that house. And I want to give that to her."

"Ah," I say gruffly. "I'm sure you're doing the right thing."

"People keep saying, 'You two are so young.' We're getting that a lot."

"Fuck 'em," somebody says.

"But that's what Matty *won't* be doing," Jason points out. "He's gonna fuck one person for the rest of his life. And that's why we all look a little freaked out when we talk about marriage."

I don't agree. Fucking one person forever doesn't scare me at all. I only hope I'll have that chance. But I don't say that, because I don't want to draw any attention to myself. Yet. Instead, I wave down the server and order another pint of the special ale. Maybe nerves have killed off my tolerance for alcohol, because I am already feeling the one beer.

"Graham, my man," Jason says beside me. "You've got some explaining to do."

Oh boy. "Is that right?" I ask, feeling everyone's attention land on me.

"Yeah, man. Your team goes to the Frozen Four, and we don't hear about it from you? Where is the smack talk? Or do you think it's enough to just grace us with your heroic presence?"

I grin, loosening up at this temporary reprieve. "You know I didn't play in any of those championship games last year, right? I got a serious concussion right before the post-season."

"That sucks, man."

"It did. Still, it was a trip watching my guys make headlines." *My guys.* One in particular, especially.

"Why aren't you playing this year?" Jason asks. "Your head is okay now, right?"

"Sure," I say slowly. "There were a few reasons. Recovering from that head injury was a bitch. It could have wrecked my academic semester. And if you get a second concussion it can take even longer to heal. Also, I wanted to take a job editing the sports section of my campus paper. That gamble will hopefully pay off in job interviews at sports networks."

"That could be a fun permanent job," Newman admits.

"Could be," I agree. "If I find something."

"Are we gonna see you on TV calling the games?" someone asks.

"You never know." The moment lingers and I wonder what to say next. *And also guys I'm totally gay! Group hug!* I feel a little bubble of hysteria rise in my chest.

So I swallow down another gulp of this excellent beer.

"All right," Matty Newman says. "I'll be the one who bring this up…"

I brace myself.

"That gay guy who made the news on your team last year—John Rikker. I remember him from freshman year. What was *that* like, when he showed up at Harkness?"

"Um…" I actually laugh, and I can feel my face getting red. "Now there's a story."

"Hell of a player he turned out to be," somebody mutters.

"Sure, but who knew we had a fag on our team?" Jerry Bakey asks.

I lift a hand in the air. "Hang on now. Let's not break out the slurs, shall we?" I look Bakey in the eye, though I'm starting to sweat.

The server takes that moment to return, plunking a pint glass down in front of me. I curl my hand around its chilly surface and try to feel calm.

"Didn't mean nothing by it," Bakey says.

"Good to know," I say, then wait a few seconds for the rest of the beers to land on the table. When the server leaves, I clear my throat. "John Rikker *is* a hell of a player. He's also my boyfriend."

Newman's pint glass hits the table with a bang, and the sound is followed immediately by his laughter. "Way to stir the pot, Graham. Good one. I've missed you."

A couple of other guys laugh, too, while my heart does a frantic dance inside my chest. I take a deep drink of my beer and then sigh.

"Holy shit," Jason says slowly. "Wait. Were you kidding, or not?"

I shake my head.

Silence falls swiftly. Everyone stares. It's the perfect opportunity to say something breezy. If only I knew what that was. I've just spent the better part of two years learning to tell the truth, whatever the cost. But as the silence thickens, I realize these friends are the least likely to stick with me. Unlike my Harkness teammates, we don't have any meaningful contact anymore, and that makes it harder for them to feel comfortable.

And still—if this bunch is the worst of my collateral damage, I'll take it.

"So…" Jason says slowly. "You're…"

"Gay." Rikker would cheer to hear me say it so plainly.

"Like, for r-real?" Newman stutters.

"That is correct. Always have been," I add. With my free hand, I trace the outline of my car keys in my pocket, wondering if I'll be leaving abruptly. I should have stopped at one beer. That was bad planning.

More silence and gaping stares.

"But…" Jason continues, not ready to let it go. "You screwed

Harper's twin sister on prom night. That's what she told everyone, anyway."

The pressure must have been getting to me because a bark of laughter escapes my chest. "True story."

"I don't get it," Jason insists. He doesn't look angry or disgusted, though. Just very confused.

My finger takes another trip around the rim of my pint glass. "Spent a really long time trying to be straight, that's all. But it doesn't work like that."

"Christ," Newman says. "What did your parents say? Do they know?"

"Yeah. Took me a long time to tell them, and then I wished I'd done it sooner. My parents are great," I add. "Anyway. That's my news. Didn't expect you all to be real excited about it, but there it is. Too bad this place doesn't serve shots," I joke.

The jaws around the table still hang open. Two guys won't look me in the eye. Bakey, for one. But Newman lifts his glass in my direction. "I think Graham just won the night, guys. And here I thought my engagement was a shocker."

Most people laugh and join in the toast. A couple don't.

But I've done it. Telling them the truth has left me sweaty and shaking with adrenaline. But I've done it, nonetheless. I take a deep gulp of my beer in celebration.

Another coming-out moment survived.

CHAPTER 6
RIKKER

I'VE MADE it about half a block down the street when two things happen. First, my phone buzzes with a new text. Second, as I reach to retrieve it from my pocket, my father's Camry rolls slowly toward me on the street. He's on his way home from work.

Shit.

The car pulls over to the curb, and the window rolls down. "John? Something wrong?"

Why yes, there is.

I walk over to the car and peer into the window. "I'm sorry," I say, then kick myself. This shit just isn't my fault. "Mom invited Pastor VanderBeek over for dinner. I asked her whether there was some kind of agenda there. She said yes. They want to talk about therapy."

My father's face falls. "I didn't know she would do that."

"I know," I say, certain he's telling the truth. "But she did it anyway."

"Get in," my dad urges, reaching across to pull the handle on the passenger door.

"Uh, I can't, okay? I was fine with silence, but I don't need to hear that man shame me to my face."

"Just get in so I can talk to you for a second." He turns the key, cutting the engine to prove his intentions.

So I do it. I slide onto the passenger seat, my bag at my feet, and we sit parked in front of a stranger's house, both silent for a moment.

"Look. I understand if you can't stay," he says.

"You do?"

"Yes, okay? *Yes.* I get it. Your mother isn't going about this the right way."

"Going about *what?*" I demand. "You can't change me, and I don't want to be changed." My throat closes up on the last word, leaving me to gulp audibly. For the first time in ages, I feel out of control.

"I'm not going to try to change you," he says quietly. "I...did some reading. Those therapies don't work, and they're cruel."

The pressure builds inside my chest. "No kidding. But it pisses me off that you'd *want* to change me. That's not what parents are supposed to do." *You're just supposed to love me.*

Right. Dream on.

Dad lets out a sigh. "I can't say that I wouldn't have chosen a different path for you. Don't forget that my introduction to the topic was finding you bloody in a hospital bed. What parent wants that?"

I make an angry noise. "That's a cop-out. It shouldn't matter that my life got a little ugly there for a minute. That was just bad luck. You don't get to tell me that you wish the world was different, and then drive my ass out of state to solve the problem. 'Better sprint out of town with our pervert kid so nobody knows.'"

My father's chin drops. "I'm sorry if I ever made you feel like a dirty secret."

"But you're still doing it! If you want me to come home and eat taco bake, I shouldn't have to lie to do it. Either I'm your son and you can say that out loud, or I'm not. It's your call."

"You are my son," he says quickly. "I accept you. But I don't know how to get your mother to do the same."

"I don't trust it." Shit. The truth just keeps falling out of my mouth. "If you accept me, then you should be able to tell her how it is."

"I *have,*" he says with a sharpness I'm not expecting. "But she won't engage. And so I'm just stumped. When I married your mother, I said, 'Until death do us part.' I made a vow. There's no exception for when your spouse is wrong, John. Seven years ago we had a crisis, and I didn't like any of your mother's solutions."

A chill snakes up my back. "What did she want to do with me?"

He tosses his head as if shaking off the memory. "It doesn't matter now. I knew she was wrong. So I did the best thing I could at the time. I put you in the car and I drove you to the person that I trust most in the *world*." My father's voice is shaking now. "And she was so good for you. When we walked in the door of your grandmother's home, she smiled like your bruised face was the most beautiful thing she'd ever seen." He swipes at his eyes with the back of one hand.

And now mine are damp, too.

"…so I knew I'd done something right. I left you in her care. Then I came home to work on your mother. I thought she needed just a little time to get over her shock. That she'd calm down and make the right decision. But it backfired. You were out of her sight, and she rewrote the story in a way that was easier for her to accept. And meanwhile, you were doing so well. You had a new hockey team and good grades. Friends. Your grandmother made sure to tell me all the nice things that happened to you."

"I had a boyfriend," I say, wondering if he can say that word aloud.

"Yes," he says quietly. "Skippy. I knew that, too. So even though I failed you at home, I knew you were okay. I'd done one little thing right. And I let myself believe it was enough. I'm sorry if I ever made you think I didn't care."

My eyes leak. We sit there in silence for a couple of minutes, just taking up space and feeling like shit.

I never should have come here.

"I'll take you wherever you want to go now," my father says eventually. "You're right that there's no reason why you need to listen to VanderBeek's bullshit. We could go out for a beer somewhere together."

"I'm going to stay with Graham," I say, clearing my throat. "I already texted him." I haven't actually communicated with him yet, but it doesn't matter. When someone loves you, they're always ready for you.

I pull out my phone and find his response. *At Founders Brewing Co with HS hockey team. Miss you.*

"Can you drive me to Founders?" I ask. "That's where G is, and I've never been to that place."

My dad lets out a disappointed sigh. "All right. But I hope you'll say goodbye before you go on Thursday."

I don't make any promises.

He puts the car in gear and starts her up.

It's a twenty-minute drive, and I spend it thinking about Graham and how happy he'll be that I have a couple of extra days to spend with him.

The car is silent until the moment my father pulls up in front of the giant brewery building.

"Wow," I say, eyeing the place. "They must print money in this place."

"I'm sure that's true." When I open the car door, my father grips my forearm. "One second, okay?"

Slowly, I turn back to face him.

"What can I do for you?" he asks.

"Uh…" I glance at the bar, wishing myself inside. I'm so close to freedom, and I don't know how to interpret his question.

"Next time we see each other, how about I visit you?" he suggests. "I could come to one of your games in the fall."

"Okay," I say quickly. A visit on my own turf sounds about a thousand times better than this debacle.

"What else?"

"The tuition you've been paying," I blurt out. "I want my degree, and I appreciate your help with the part that financial aid doesn't cover."

"Of course. That's a given."

Hearing that brings my blood pressure down more than a few notches. "That's really all I need, I guess. For now. I'll spend next summer with Gran again. It's my last chance before I graduate in a year."

"One more year," he says.

"Yeah. Pretty hard to believe."

He actually smiles. "Please take care of yourself. Call my cell if there's something else I can do for you."

"All right. Thanks." I wrench my bag off the floor of the car and push the door open wider.

"Hey."

I look back one more time after getting out.

"I'm proud of you."

Shit! My eyes well up immediately. "Thanks," I say, giving him an awkward wave before shutting the door. Then I'm standing there on the sidewalk in front of a giant brew pub, my eyes like fountains.

Because I'd needed to hear that so very badly.

I wait until my dad drives off down the street. Then I take a deep breath and begin a slow trip around the building. The brewery takes up an entire city block. By the time I make it to the entrance, the cold winter air has dried my eyes. They're probably red, though.

Graham won't care.

"Enjoy," the bouncer says after checking my ID.

"Thanks."

CHAPTER 7
GRAHAM

THE STRESS MAKES ME STRESSY.

No.

Wait.

The stress makes me sloppy. Like, seriously. With just three pints of the special ale in me, I'm already slurring. Or I will be if I decide to say anything.

I just sit here drinking the special, getting blurry. But it's not every day you tell your former hockey team you need a good dicking down.

Wait.

No, I didn't say that.

But I do. Need one, that is.

Blergh.

Suddenly, the special special ale develops some righteous hallucinogenic powers. I look up and Rik is standing across the room, trying to make eye contact with me.

I stand up so fast the beer glasses on the table rattle.

"Whoa, there," Jason says, steadying his glass.

Rikker's beautiful mouth is curved into a guarded smile. He starts walking toward me, but I can't wait. I take a couple of steps toward him and sort of launch myself in his direction.

Or rather, I try to. But drunk legs don't always go where you've planned. My aim is off, and my hug is going to miss its target. Rik sort of catches me before I tumble. The hug I've planned becomes more like an aerial rescue.

"Wow," he says, bracing me against his strong, delectable chest. "Easy, killer." Gently, he sets me onto my feet then takes a step back.

I'm disappointed until I see him eyeing the table of hockey players behind me. We have an audience, damn it. And it's me who always refuses PDA. Rikker is just watching out for me. As always.

But why is he here? I want to ask, but a giant beer belch stops my progress.

Rik's eyes widen. And they're kind of blurry. *Someone* is blurry. It might be me.

"Hey," I say stupidly.

"Hey, yourself. You okay?"

"I'm…the special."

Everyone laughs all at once, including Rikker.

"Uh, okay," he says, his gaze giving everyone else a once-over. "Hi guys. Remember me?"

"Kinda," Matty Newman says. "But we got a refresher on your life a little while ago."

"*Really*," Rikker says, his expression cautious again.

"Congrats on your division championship last year."

"Thanks?" He looks me up and down. "You got wasted and then got confessional?"

I turn my finger in a circle. "Other way around. Not sure why I'm so…" *Burp.*

"It's the special ale," Jason says. "It's fifteen percent alcohol."

"*Fifteen?*" Rikker and I say in unison. He leans over and lifts my nearly empty glass off the table. He takes a sip. "So that's, like, two or three times as potent as a normal beer."

"That explains a lot," I say slowly, careful to articulate each word. "Want one?" I ask. "Sit?" Short sentences work better right now.

The rest of the guys sort of shake off their surprise. Chairs scrape against the floor as they make room for Rikker.

Still, he hesitates. "Sure? I didn't mean to crash."

I narrow my eyes at him. "What are you doing here, anyway? I thought you were hanging with the parents?"

"Not so much." His shoulders slump. "I'll fill you in on that later."

"Oh fuck." And now I notice the suitcase in his hand.

"Whatever. Hey—did you eat anything?"

I shake my head.

He puts his hands on my shoulders and steers me gently toward my empty chair. "Sit. Let me find you some food, because I think you need it. Anyone else want anything?"

Newman stands up. "Should I just make this simple and order a burger for everyone?"

"Sure," Jason says, tossing a twenty dollar bill toward Newman.

Feeling a little more sober, I watch Rikker walk toward the food window with Newman. "So you played for Michigan State, right?" Rikker is saying. "You must know Jared Smith."

"Sure do…"

As they move out of earshot, I'm admiring Rikker's muscular ass in a pair of well-worn khaki pants. It's just occurring to me that his troubles at home mean that I've gained two extra days in his company. And I am…wasted.

Bummer.

"So…" Jason says. "You're, like, a couple? Really?"

"Yeah. He won't graduate this spring, though," I slur. "We might be long distance."

Jason looks from Rikker to me once more and then frowns. "Still don't quite get it."

"S'okay." I shrug. "Took me a while, too."

He laughs, but I'm dead serious. "Do people give you shit sometimes? Is that why you stopped playing hockey?"

I shake my head. "It's complicated. People can be dicks. But you figure out pretty quick who your real friends are. And everybody who doesn't treat you like a leper, you're grateful for those people. It makes you a better friend to them."

"Yeah, all right. That makes sense." He nods slowly.

Rikker and Newman come back a few minutes later, with two trays heavy with burgers and fries. Rikker uncaps a bottle of water and hands it to me. "Drink this."

I do.

"Now eat this," he says, passing me a plate.

Half a dozen hockey players eye us as if we're about to start humping in public, or something.

I'm too drunk to care. I eat the burger and never take my eyes off Rikker.

CHAPTER 8
RIKKER

AFTER A GOOD BURGER AND FRIES, I feel more optimistic about humanity than I did before.

When the hockey team party breaks up, I take Graham's keys and prepare to drive his family Subaru back to the suburb where we grew up. "Should we call your parents and give 'em a heads-up?" I ask in the parking lot. "Your mom wasn't expecting a guest."

Graham shakes his head sloppily. "They're out tonight. And she won't mind at all. Think she was half expecting you to turn up, anyway."

I groan. "Hope she put money on it, then."

"How bad was it?" my boyfriend asks, dropping onto the passenger's seat and pulling his door closed.

"Well..." I toss my suitcase in the backseat and then get into the driver's seat. "My dad wasn't the problem. He's been surprisingly cool. But he hasn't done a good job of corralling my mother. She invited that bigot of a pastor over tonight to try to talk me into therapy."

Graham twists toward me so fast his knee bangs into the stick shift. "No shit?"

Nodding, I start the engine. "I just walked out without saying anything. My father is probably gonna be in the doghouse for weeks for driving me over here to meet you."

"He can take it," Graham argues. "If he wanted you home so bad, he should have made sure she wouldn't do that."

"Yeah." I sigh. But for the first time I feel a little sorry for my dad. It had almost been easier to hate both of them equally. I back out of the parking spot. "Okay, don't laugh. Which way do I turn? I never really drove around downtown before."

Graham flinches. The neighborhood where I'd gotten beaten up is probably less than two miles from here. That awful day had happened right after I got my license. "Turn left. We need the highway entrance."

"Okay," I say after a minute. "This looks sort of familiar. It's trippy. Like I know this place, and I don't."

"Sorry I got so drunk," he says quietly. "Didn't mean to."

My hand crosses the gearbox to squeeze his knee. "It's not a problem. I'm proud of you for coming out to those guys. That must have been scary."

He shrugs, not wanting the praise. "I'm getting better at it."

"I know you are."

Walking into Graham's house is like walking into my past again. Only this time I don't mind. There's the kitchen table where we used to eat a whole package of cookies in one sitting. And there's the door to the basement where we used to go to play video games and make out.

"I'm putting your bag in my room," Graham says, his hand on the bannister. "Let's watch a movie. I need to sober up."

"Okay. In the den?" I don't know where Graham watches his TV these days.

"On my bed. I'll be right back to look for popcorn, unless you want to do it."

"Sure." I'm not hungry, but I open Mrs. Graham's cabinet above the toaster. Some things don't change at all in seven years. The microwave popcorn is right where it always was.

All the best parts of my early teenaged years had happened in this house and on the ice rink a mile or so from here.

Humming to myself, I put the popcorn in the nuker and throw away its plastic wrapper. I check my phone and find a text message from Trevi, the Harkness team captain. *My sister knitted me another pair of socks for Christmas. Want to bet on whether Big-D calls them gay?*

There's a photo attached, and it makes me laugh. The socks are a painfully bright orange.

I'm sure your sister loves you. But she hides it well, I reply.

No kidding. DJ got socks in a nice, soothing navy. How's your vacation?

Standing in G's kitchen right now making popcorn. It could be worse. As I tap this out, I realize it's true. Even if the day has been an emotional shit show, I'm going to be okay. *You?*

Heading out to a pickup hockey game.

Have fun!

I dump the popcorn in one of Mrs. G's bowls. Then I grab two cans of Coke out of the well-stocked refrigerator and carry everything upstairs. Graham's room isn't very familiar to me, because we'd always hung out in his basement when we were young. His room is also a shrine to high school, I notice. There are hockey trophies on the bookshelf, much like the ones in my Vermont bedroom.

I make myself at home on the bed and turn on his TV, wondering what we should watch.

Graham emerges from the bathroom a minute later, wiping his face with a towel. "You pick something?"

I haven't. "*Diablo*?"

"We looked at that one before." Graham frowns. "Weren't the reviews terrible? You're in a Scott Eastwood mood, huh?"

"I might be." I look down at his serene face. His eyes are closed even as he argues with me. "I don't care what movie we watch. I just want to sit here with you and think about nothing."

He opens one eye. "That's all you want to do?"

"Well…" I chuckle. "I can think of some other fun activities I could get up to with your big drunk self. But your parents could show up at any point, right?"

"Yup." He sighs, relaxing against me. "Pick a movie. You don't even have to tell me what it is."

The warm weight of him feels great against my chest, and I sift my fingers through his dark-blond hair. Then I choose a movie.

"What the fuck?" Graham sputters a minute or so later when he realizes that I've picked *The Longest Ride*. "This is a chick flick."

"Scott Eastwood riding bulls, though."

He laughs so hard he gurgles into my abs.

"Breathe, dude." I rub his back. "It's not *that* funny."

"It is!" He wraps his arms around my waist and howls.

"Mmm. Lower," I encourage.

Still chuckling, he kisses the fly of my jeans. Then he does it again, the tease.

"Kiss me, fool."

His smiling mouth lifts to find mine. And—drunk or not—Graham's kiss is sweet and hot. He presses his delectable hips against mine and tilts his head. "Mmm," he breathes as his lips make the perfect connection.

Indeed.

I open for him, sliding my tongue between his lips. He tastes like toothpaste and comfort. His big hands grip my body as our kisses grow deeper. It isn't frantic, though. When we were teens, making out was a sweaty dash to the finish line. Our sixteen-year-old selves were too desperate to get off to savor each kiss.

But we're older and wiser now. Both rhythmic and lazy. This is the good part, too.

With my arms around Graham, I roll us to the side. Our bodies line up so perfectly and our movie is forgotten. Hands skim and caress. My dick is pretty excited about bumping against Graham's, but the rest of me is more relaxed than I've been all week. Everything is finally okay.

I love you, my kisses say.

I know, is his reply. And then Graham's kisses slow down, his body lolling against mine.

"You're falling asleep kissing me, aren't you?"

"Not all the way," he mumbles.

Laughing, I tuck him against my side, the back of my hand stroking his drunk face. He lets out a contented sigh.

We have all night. So I turn my attention back to the movie. Scott

Eastwood and the earnest little college student spend a lot of time staring into each other's eyes.

It's a little dull, to be honest.

"Hey," I say, jiggling Graham a little when there is finally some nudity. "Scott Eastwood, naked. Shower sex."

"Mmrrhb," Graham says. But then he shakes himself awake. He glances at the screen and perks up even more. "Now we're talking."

But he doesn't watch. He moves the bowl of popcorn off the bed, and then lifts my shirt. Two seconds later his lips are teasing the skin just below my belly button. And his hand is fumbling with the button on my khakis.

"Well, hello to you, too," I say happily. Since I'm still holding the remote, I pause the movie and concentrate on what's really important —Graham's mouth near my cock. He's teasing me a little—kissing my stomach and slowly unzipping me. Even when that's done, he only strokes me over my briefs, his fingers teasing me through the cotton.

I push my fingers through his golden hair and sigh. My hips roll eagerly and he chuckles.

"You're still drunk, aren't you?"

"Yep," he says between kisses. "S'nice."

Yes, it is. I reach down and adjust myself, which has the benefit of making the tip of my erection visible.

Graham takes the hint, lapping at me with his tongue. But he's still making me wait for more, because he knows it makes me crazy.

Really, things could be worse.

"Michael? Are you still up?" The sound of Mrs. Graham's voice cuts through my happy, horny reverie.

I'm basically stunned like a deer in the road. But Graham reacts, sitting up fast, grabbing the popcorn bowl and planting it squarely over my unzipped crotch. The jerky movement flings a few kernels of popcorn overboard, though.

As her face appears in the open doorway, I grab the remote and try to look innocent.

Her eyebrows lift in surprise at the sight of me on the bed with Graham. "Johnny!" she whispers. "Hi, honey!"

"Hi, Mrs. G!" I give her a big, awkward smile.

Her eyes flit toward the screen, where Scott Eastwood's wet, naked body is frozen in HD. "Good movie?" she asks, and I can hear the humor in her voice.

"Eh," I say. "It has its moments."

"I was fixing to have cookies and tea, if anyone's interested," she says. "I just need to take off these heels."

"Great plan," I agree sheepishly.

As she disappears, I think I can hear her chuckling.

Downstairs, I dip pieces of a chocolate chip cookie in milk while Mrs. G asks me questions, first about myself and then about Graham, who declined to come down with us. "You're sure he's okay?"

"Yeah. I'm sure."

"His old friends weren't awful?"

"Didn't seem like it. A little surprised, maybe."

She stirs her tea, a worried expression on her face. "This town doesn't make it easy. As much as I'd like to have Michael nearby after graduation, I understand why he's applying for jobs in big cities."

"That's where the jobs are," I point out.

"I hope this interview in D.C. works out for him."

"D.C.?" I know nothing about this.

She winces. "He just got the email. Hasn't even set a date for the interview. I'm sure he was going to tell you about it."

"Sure," I echo lamely.

D.C. is awfully far from Harkness. I keep hoping he'll get something in New York, which is just a commuter-rail trip away from Harkness, Connecticut. Visiting him next year could get expensive.

Ah, well. No point in worrying about it yet.

"How was your Christmas?" I ask, steering her from the topic.

She tells me about the pageant at her new church, with the live donkey for Mary to ride. "The sanctuary smells like a barnyard now, but it was quite impressive." She smiles at me. "Honey, you look tired. I should let you go to sleep."

"That's probably a good idea," I admit. This day needs to end right away. "Okay if I take Lori's room?"

"You can do that, or stay in Michael's room. Whatever you want."

That's nice of her to say, except for one problem. "He's a roller, though." And that bed in his room is only a double. At school we have two twins pushed together into a makeshift king-sized bed. But even a queen-size is dicey with Graham.

"Still?" She cackles. "When we went on family vacations, we'd flip coins to see who had to share a hotel bed with him."

"That doesn't surprise me at all," I say, getting to my feet and gathering up my milk glass and used napkin.

Mrs. G corners me near the sink where I'm putting my glass into her dishwasher. "I'm so sorry your visit didn't go smoothly, honey. I would do anything to make it easier for you."

I close the dishwasher and turn around. "It's really okay," I say quietly.

"No." She shakes her head. "It really isn't."

"But I'm okay," I clarify.

She doesn't argue. She just hugs me.

CHAPTER 9
GRAHAM

IN THE MORNING, I wake up alone.

Groggy and mildly head-achey, I get up to brush my teeth and drink cup after cup of water. When I'm finished, I stand in the upstairs hallway, listening to the sounds in the house. My father is gone to work already, and Mom's podcasts are playing downstairs.

The door to my sister's bedroom is shut, so I walk past it and go downstairs.

"There's coffee," Mom says. She's seated at the kitchen table, a shopping list in front of her. "What should I make for dinner?"

"Steak?" I suggest hopefully. It's a splurge.

"Sure," she says immediately. "With mashed potatoes and roasted broccoli. And chocolate cake!" She looks up and smiles at me. "That would cheer anyone up, right?"

My heart turns to mush, because I know just what she's up to. "Mom, John is okay."

"I know," she says, scribbling on her shopping list. "But I'm going to spoil him anyway. Someone should." She caps her pen and stands up. "Any last requests? I'm heading to D&W."

"I'm sure you thought of everything."

"Want to come along?" she tries. "You could pick out a red wine that goes with steak."

"Like I'd know which one goes with steak. I'll shower instead."

"Fine." She kisses me on the cheek. "Back in a jif. I hope you'll let John sleep."

"Of course I will," I assure her, pouring myself a cup of coffee.

The minute her car rolls down the driveway, I leave the cup on the counter and head back upstairs. I tiptoe toward my sister's bedroom. Inside, Rikker is asleep, face down in Lori's bed, his strong arms framing his mussed head.

That's all the invitation I need. I lock the door and drop all my clothes on the rug, then slip into bed with him.

Having my boyfriend sleep over is all new territory. A year ago I would have burst into flames at the thought of getting naked at home with Rik. But now I'm kissing his bare back and running my hands through his messy hair.

Have I come a long way, or what?

He lets out a sleepy groan. But then his warm hand reaches up to skim my arm with happy fingers.

As I study long eyelashes pointing down at his handsome cheekbones, my heart breaks just a little more. This man's mother can't love him just the way he is? There is nobody more beautiful. She's just insane.

There are moms all over the world struggling to help their violent sons, or drug-addicted sons. Or lazy ones. John Rikker is a hardworking, successful, handsome man. He's a good friend, a loving grandson, and a generous lover. There is nothing in the world I wouldn't do for him.

His eyelids flutter open. He squints up at me. "Everything okay?" he whispers.

My voice is low and husky. "So much better than okay. Mom just went to the grocery store."

He gives me a sleepy smile, and his feet find mine under the covers. "We're home alone, huh?"

"For thirty minutes, at least."

"It'll have to do," he says with a lazy smile. "Just like high school, right?"

"Right." We share a conspiratorial grin. There's never been a more perfect moment than this one. We're safe and together. That's all I ever wanted. "You know what the most exciting moment of my life was?"

"No," he whispers, brushing my pecs with his palm. "Tell me."

"In the basement, sophomore year of high school…"

His smile grows wider, because we did a lot of surreptitious fooling around in the basement.

"…my mother left for a shift volunteering at the church supper." I move closer and cup his face, my thumb stroking his cheekbone.

"That wasn't the first time we fooled around," he whispers.

"I know." As if I could ever forget. Our first kiss was an accident, right in the middle of a wrestling match. Our second kisses happened when my mother went to the grocery store. "It was our third time." I lean in and press a kiss to his lips. It's mostly chaste, but slow. I want to really feel the slide of my lips over his warm ones.

"Why was the third time so exciting?" he asks, and we're so close I can feel his breath on my skin.

"Because…" I let the back of my hand brush his bare chest, before sifting through his happy trail. "It's the first time you ever put your hand down my pants."

His eyes take on an amused glint as I tease his abs with my knuckles.

"I'm not kidding," I whisper, tracing the skin just above the elastic on his briefs. "You slipped your hand…" I breach the elastic and slide my own hand slowly down, avoiding his dick, just touching his belly as it descends into his groin. "Right here. I was dying, wanting your touch so bad. Going out of my mind while you kissed me."

Our lips meet again, and this time the kiss is hot and sweet. Our teeth click as we both lean in for more. His pubic hair tickles my fingertips. His moan is so quiet that I feel it more than I hear it.

"And then you took me in hand," I say, finally wrapping my hand around his girth. The hot weight of him against my palm is everything. All these years later, I'm still amazed at how he makes me feel. "Just like this." My thumb sweeps over his tip and he hisses, his head tipping back. "I nearly came on the spot. Nobody had ever touched me before. I wanted it so bad."

Rikker reaches for me, finding lots of bare skin. "Can't believe you're naked right now," he whispers against my lips. "Can we be quick?"

"We'll be qui—" I can't even finish the sentence because he wraps a hand around my cock, and I moan instead.

He pushes me onto my back, then climbs on top of me, kicking his underwear out of the way. Our mouths fuse for a kiss that's deep and dirty. Skin to skin, we began to move, our dicks sliding together. The weight of his body on mine is delicious. "We never did *this* in your basement," he whispers.

Unghh. "Woulda blown my poor little mind."

Rikker smiles down at me, warmth in his eyes. His family is cruel, but that smile never dies. If I were ever as strong as Rikker, I'd be a worthy man.

He takes my mouth in another hungry kiss. I sink into the bed and spread my legs, letting him urge me closer to orgasm. Usually we try to make it last. But today—just like in high school—the need for stealth and a quick release wins out.

The bed thumps once against the wall as he picks up the pace. Rikker stretches out his arm and braces it against the wall, preventing a repeat of that sound. I'm caged beneath him, held in place by his arms and his muscular body.

My favorite place in the world.

Rik's breathing quickens. I love that sound—proof that I have the same effect on him as he does on me. His lips track from my mouth to my ear. "Baby," he says so softly that I only hear the "B" sounds.

I slap his hip, giving him a nudge. He makes room for my hand between our bodies. I wrap my hand around us both, as best I can. Rik is leaking for me. I slide my thumb through his slickness and feel all his muscles tense. He buries his face in my neck and shudders, erupting into my hand in hot bursts.

And...*winning!* My slick hand needs only a couple more strokes before I push my head back into the pillow and come hard.

Yesssss. Achievement unlocked.

Breathing hard, I lay back and smile up at my boyfriend. "Good morning."

He kisses me on the nose. "We made a mess."

"Totally worth it," I whisper back. "Had to do what I can to save your shitty week."

The next kiss I get is on the mouth, and it's a good one. "It wasn't so shitty."

"Seriously?"

He shakes his head. "I've been dreading this trip. The conflict. Now I don't have to anymore. And I found out my dad is a little more solid than I thought. Your high school teammates aren't superturds. And you're cute when you're accidentally wasted. Your mom fed me cookies, just like old times. And *then* we fooled around. I've had worse weeks."

"Superturds?"

He grins.

"I don't know how you do it."

"Do what?"

"Stay so fucking cheery. I've come a long way, but you're in a whole different league."

In answer, he leans down and licks my cheek. Now, there are hot moments in bed when that would be super sexy. But this is more like being slobbered on by a St. Bernard. I squirm, and he laughs. "Get up."

"We're sticky."

"Yeah, I noticed. Let's have a quick shower." He sits up.

I swing my legs off the bed and open the door to Lori's en suite bathroom. My parents actually gave my sister the master bedroom because she and I used to fight over her extraordinary use of the other bathroom. I hated her for it. It's really handy right now, though.

"Come here. Time's a wasting." I pull the curtain back and turn on the water. As soon as it warms up, I hop in and wet my hair.

Rikker follows me. "You know that barely took the edge off." He runs his hands all over my chest. "Any chance your parents are going out again tonight? To, say, a four-hour opera?"

I laugh, getting water up my nose. "Not likely. Mom is making you a steak dinner and chocolate cake."

"Really?" Wordlessly, we switch sides of the shower so that he can have a turn under the water. "Did you tell her not to be so worried?" He puts his handsome face under the spray.

"Oh, I did. But I can't control her. And who am I to say no to steak and cake?"

He puts a possessive hand on my ass and squeezes. "I guess this will have to wait."

"Stop. I don't want to spend the whole day trying to hide my boner."

"I know exactly where I want to hide mine," he says with a sigh.

And I laugh.

CHAPTER 10
RIKKER

FINALLY, we're in the car, headed for Chicago. It's my rental, but Graham is driving. I'm staring out the window at the dirty snow-banks, feeling blue.

"It was nice of your dad to buy us breakfast," Graham says quietly.

"Yeah," I grunt. "I mean, no. Isn't it the least he can do?" We've just left the cafe where he'd met us for eggs and conversation.

It was stilted, everyone trying too hard. I'd survived it, but I'm just *done* with this place. I want to reach over and press Graham's leg down on the accelerator. The faster we leave town, the more normal I'll feel.

"Your dad tried," Graham says gently. "He was nice to me."

"Yeah," I admit with a sigh. "He was."

The car eats up more highway toward Chicago. And even though I'm almost free of Michigan, it still hangs over me like a cloud. The place will never feel like home again. It will always make me feel like the penguin chick left to die in the ravine.

"Will it be weird to be at Skippy's wedding?" Graham asks care-fully, after another of my long silences.

"What?" I haven't thought about Skippy for days. Even though he is my ex. "No. I mean—no weirder than any other wedding. Why?"

He shrugs. "The road not taken."

"Oh, I drove that road all the way to its end. He's Ross's problem now." I chuckle. "Will it be weird for you?"

"Nah," he says easily. "No weirder than any other wedding." He turns to give me a quick smile. "Remind me why it's in Chicago?"

"Skippy has an older sister, and her husband owns the venue. Skippy is getting his wedding reception basically for free, because the hotel just got a big renovation and it hasn't reopened all the way yet."

"Handy," Graham says.

"Yeah, if you're into that kind of thing." The idea of planning a wedding is so foreign to me. Spending my life with someone isn't, though. And that reminds me of something else I'm grumpy about. "G, your mom said you got an interview in Washington, D.C."

He nods quickly. "Right. I haven't even set it up yet."

"Were you going to tell me?"

"Yeah." He sighs. "D.C. is still a long shot, though. And I was hoping to tell you I'd gotten a job offer close to Harkness."

"You shouldn't factor that in when you're choosing a job." I play that back in my head and wince. "I mean—I'm only in Connecticut for one more year. Nine months, really. It's not enough time to plan your life around."

"I like New York, though," he says. "And the Rangers are looking at you."

"We might as well buy a lottery ticket," I grumble. "What are the odds of me playing for the Rangers?"

"Good, actually," he says calmly. "Do you not want me in New York?"

"Of *course* I do." But it comes out sounding angry. "I just wouldn't want you to rein in your search. You should take the most amazing job you can find, no matter where."

Now it's Graham who goes silent. It's so quiet in the car that the engine noise is all I hear. We roll forward for a few miles, and I wonder why I'm fucking everything up. "If you got a job in New York, that would be pretty cool," I say. "But I'll come see you wherever you are."

I reach across the console and put my hand on his thigh. "You can count on that."

"Can I?" he asks, voice strained. "You don't really talk about life after graduation. But it's all I can think about right now."

"I don't talk about it because we don't know what it looks like yet. But I'll still want to be with you, G."

"You say that," he says slowly. "But you've done long distance before, and I know you didn't like it much."

I prop my elbow against the window, and then put my forehead into my palm. I don't even know why we're having this depressing conversation right now. "It's not easy, I'll give you that. But it's not impossible."

There's another strained silence that I fear might last forever. But then Graham puts on the turn signal and takes the next exit. He pulls into a truck-stop gas station, so I expect him to get out and take a pee break. But he just kills the engine and turns to me. "Listen," he says. "I know the timing is terrible, and you're kind of a mess today. But there's something I have to say."

"What is it?" I ask as ice slides into my gut, because I don't like the sound of that.

"I've been trying to figure this job thing out without involving you. I wanted to have it all solved and bring you a plan. 'Here's where I'm working and here's what we'll do.' Because I didn't want to give you any reason to say, 'You know, maybe it's just better if we go our separate ways.'"

"But…"

He holds up a hand. "And I haven't always found it easy to say how I feel, because I don't want to be rejected. But here goes. I love you, and I'm never going to stop. Not even if the only job I find is in Alaska. I love you and I want to be with you, no matter how hard it is. And I will wait for you to sort out your own shit as long as it takes. Any questions?"

"No," I croak, because there's suddenly a giant lump in my throat. "Wait, I got one. How did you become the high-functioning person in this relationship?"

Graham lets out a burst of nervous laughter. "I know, right?" He turns toward me on the seat. "Come here." I lean in, letting him wrap me into a hug. "Everything I know I learned from you."

"Not true," I say, trying to swallow. This has been the most emotionally overwrought week of my life.

"It is so. Now let's go to Chicago so we can blow off some steam by doing a couple other things you taught me."

"Now you're talking." I pat him on the back and take a deep breath. "Just in case it needs saying, I love you, and I want to make it work no matter what."

He doesn't let go yet. "Hang in there, Rik. Everything is just fine."

"I know," I promise him. And I even believe it. "Can I drive for a while? I need something to do besides brood."

"Sure," he says, unlatching his seatbelt. "But the reason I wanted to drive was so that I could speed. I have a serious need to get you into that hotel room ahead of schedule."

"Do you, now?" I extract myself from the car, and we pass each other by the rear fender. It's hard to miss the hungry look that Graham gives me.

"Drive hard," he says, after we settle in and buckle up. "And then you can really *drive hard*."

I pull out of there in a big hurry. Now I definitely have something better to do than brood.

CHAPTER 11
RIKKER

THE HOTEL IS cute and funky, with colorful modern furniture in the lobby, and a banner announcing a cocktail hour for Skippy's and Ross's guests at six p.m.

This means we still have time to attend to some important business first.

"Here's the key to the mini bar," says a smiley attendant behind the desk. "Here's a map of the neighborhood—"

"Thanks so much," I say, grabbing the key card off the counter.

"Would you like help with your bags?"

"Nope! Got 'em!" Graham says, eyeing the bank of elevators.

"Have a great stay," the attendant says, although we're halfway across the lobby by the time he's finished the sentence.

Graham punches the elevator button, then taps his foot.

We haven't been spotted yet by anyone in the wedding party. And I know we both want to keep it that way until we can go upstairs and unwind.

And by "unwind" I mean roll around on the king-sized bed together. Naked.

"Slow elevator," my boyfriend grumbles. That's all he says, but his gaze is not quiet. Those cool blue eyes sweep over me, undressing me. It's not subtle at all.

Ding!

"Yes!" Graham exhales with relief as the doors begin to slide apart.

"Grikker!" squeals a familiar voice. I look up just as Skippy leaps off the elevator ahead of Ross, his fiancé. "Omigod you're here! Did you just get in? Let Charles take those bags up for you! Come get coffee with us!" He grabs me into a fierce, tight hug.

"Great to see you," I manage as soon as my lungs reinflate. "You too, Ross."

Skippy's man gives me a friendly nod. With Skippy this amped over the wedding, Ross probably hasn't managed to get a word in since last Tuesday.

"We can't right now," Graham says forcefully. "Get coffee, I mean." He boards the elevator, bracing the doors open with one strong arm. "We have to…" He pauses.

"Make a phone call," I say at the exact same time that Graham says, "Do some shopping." There's another pause while our glances collide, wide-eyed. "He forgot his…" I try.

"Socks!" Graham finishes, as color streaks across both his cheeks.

"His socks," I say in a too bright voice. "But we're having cocktails later, right?" I kick my suitcase into the elevator. "Six o'clock?"

Graham jams his hand down on the button for the fifth floor.

"Yes!" Skippy enthuses. "Right here in the lobby. Oh! And let me help you find some socks. There's a men's store on the corner of—"

The address gets clipped as the doors slide closed. "Thank you!" I yell as the car begins to climb already. Then I laugh. "Subtle, Graham."

But he's not even listening. Instead, he flattens me against the wall, his big body muscling close as he gives me a bruising, desperate kiss. And then another one. I wrap my arms around him and give it to him as good as I get. "Finally," he grants between kisses.

The elevator slides to a halt.

"Not quite yet, babe," I say, giving him a gentle push. "Let's at least make it into the actual room." I grab my bag and hustle into the hallway, Graham at my heels.

I open the door to our room with the key card and flick on the lights. Room 504 is…

Okay, I have no idea what the room looks like. Graham grabs the suitcase out of my hand, and the duffel bag off my shoulder. "I should hang up my suit jacket," I say as he aims our bags in the general direction of a luggage rack.

But I guess he doesn't agree, because he's backing me up toward the bed.

"King-sized. Nice," I say as the backs of my knees hit the edge of the mattress, and I sit.

He grabs my Harkness Hockey jacket in two hands and pushes it off my body. "Strip," he says. "Now."

"I kind of like you bossy," I say, giving him a smile. His zipper is right there in front of me so I pop the button on his jeans and unzip him. "Come here, pushy one."

He takes a step closer and I kiss the soft skin of his belly, just over the waistband of his briefs. I turn my face to the side and rub my stubbled jaw over his beautiful skin.

Above me, Graham lets out a happy sigh. His fingers sift through my hair. "Can I get this shirt off you?" he asks quietly. "I want your skin on mine. *All* of it."

"Heck yes." I start unbuttoning, while Graham shucks off his own clothes. Every stitch. His cock juts proudly up at me already, and the sight makes my own leap to attention. "I guess you really did miss me."

"So much," he says, his voice a scrape of desire. He yanks back the covers and climbs onto the bed.

I toss my own clothes off my body and brace a knee on the mattress. "Hey, look. Now this is handy." I grab a purple box of condoms off the nightstand. *Skippy & Ross's Wedding Favors* it says.

Graham takes the box from me, shaking his head. Then he raises those serious blue eyes to mine. "Who says I want your ex to come between us?"

I snort loudly and tackle him, and now we're finally skin to skin. I bury my face in his neck and kiss the underside of his jaw. "Do you want to fuck me?"

He goes still with surprise. "Really?"

"I wouldn't joke about that."

He cranes his neck so he can see my face. "Sometime, yeah. But not right now."

"No? Why?" I know he's interested.

"Because I'm *way* too impatient right now. If anyone's getting fucked, it's me. And quickly." He lifts his hips off the bed an inch or so just to demonstrate his urgency. "Don't be shy, now."

Well, okay then. I prop myself up on an elbow and put my thumbnail under the edge of the condom box.

"Rik?" he asks, putting a big hand to my chest. "Why do we use condoms?"

Now it's my turn to be startled. "Um…because that's polite of me? You're always the one getting fucked. So I didn't want to be the one who hustles you into going without."

"Hustle me," he whispers. "I wanted to ask you before."

"Why didn't you?"

"Because…" He runs his hand down my flank and sighs. "I know we're exclusive right now and don't need them. But if there was a day coming when we weren't anymore, and then we'd have to go *back* to condoms…" He winces. "That would be a really bad day."

"Then let's never have that day," I say, leaning down to kiss his shoulder. "I can't picture a scenario where I'm still with you but also fucking anyone else. That's not how we work."

He smiles slowly. "No, it isn't. So maybe this is how we work." He takes the little box out of my hand and tosses it overboard.

I hear it land lightly on the rug. And suddenly I realize what's about to happen. "Are we totally going bare right now?"

"We totally are." He captures my face in one hand. "And I can't wait. So you'd better find some lube."

I spring off the bed like a spooked Chihuahua, and pounce on my bag. Two seconds later I'm lowering myself down onto Graham's willing body again, lunging for his mouth.

He gathers me up in two eager arms, and mission control has already locked down the launch coordinates. My kiss is fueled by fire. My hips settle onto Graham's, and I rock purposefully against him. His knees lift to hold me in place, so we can grind together.

"I will never get enough of you," I whisper against his lips.

"Try," he says, pushing his hips up off the bed. "Give it to me. Fast and messy. I've been thinking about this since I woke up this morning."

I lean in for one more searing kiss. Then I take the lube and pop the top, slicking up my fingers. I have to sit up to prep him. As my fingers begin their erotic tease, I watch Graham arch back into the pillow and groan. "More," he says. "Hurry."

"You say that now. But I think you overestimate my stamina." No condom? "I'm going to blow like the first firework on the Fourth of July."

He lets out a groan and wraps a hand around his own cock. The sight of him stroking himself doesn't do a thing for my fragile control. "Just do it already," he says, looking up at me with lust-heavy eyes.

Giving in, I line myself up. "If this is comically fast, just remember that I love you."

"How could I forget?" He lifts his hips and beckons to me.

I ease forward, holding my breath as I begin to fit us together. It's tight and hot and just as mind-bending as I expected it to be. "Oh, man. Wow. Fuck," I blabber as I work forward. "Are you okay? Everything is wow."

"Breathe, Rik." Graham bites his lip as he bears down. "Everything is okay."

I remember to exhale. And I realize he's right.

There aren't any more words spoken for a while after that. We don't need any at all.

"This is a nice room," Graham says a half hour later, as we lie in a heap in the center of the bed.

"Is it?" I pick my head up off his chest and scan the place for the first time. Then I put my head back down. "I don't even know why I looked. All I care about is the bed."

We're both quiet for a minute as Graham plays with my hair. "I don't know where next year will take me. And I hate not knowing."

"I'll bet," I sympathize. "But it's okay."

"I know. It will be."

"What's our strategy for tonight?" I ask. "There's a dinner after the cocktails. And then Skippy wants everyone to go to a bar in Boystown. But I could try to beg off. We can come back here and watch TV."

"No, let's go *out*," Graham says. "I watched enough TV over break already. My parents were all jazzed up about this multi-part BBC nature thing. Bored me silly."

"I saw the last part," I admit. "That fucking penguin chick abandoned in the ravine? I've had two dreams about it already. Paging Dr. Freud." I'm so tired of being stuck inside my own head. Graham is right—a bar is just what I need tonight.

His hands go still in my hair. "Did you watch the bonus episode? The 'Making Of' part?"

"What? Of the nature thing? Fuck no."

"The camera man saves it."

"What?" I lift my face to his.

Graham tilts his head to study me for a second before he speaks. "The camera man couldn't stand it, either. There's some footage of him picking up the chick and chasing its mother. He puts it down and then backs away. And the mother penguin gets it back."

"Oh. No shit?" My voice actually cracks, and I swallow hard. "That was nice of him."

"Rik." Graham's arms lock around me. "You're going to be okay."

"I'm fine," I say quickly. But my eyes are stinging. Fucking eyes.

"Uh-huh," he agrees gently. I put my head back down on his chest, and his broad hand smooths the skin of my back. "I love you. So much."

"I love you, too." I let my eyes fall shut as he continues to rub my back.

"I'll never stop."

"Okay," I agree shakily.

"Except in half an hour we have to get up and pretend to go buy some socks."

I laugh into his hug. "Right. Sure."

"Maybe we can find some with penguins on them."

"Oh, stop it."

He kisses my head and I relax against his big body. I feel happier than I have in a month. Maybe ever.

And I really am okay.

T h e
E n d

Made in United States
North Haven, CT
02 November 2024

59777673R00129